William Shakespeare's Cymbeline: A Retelling in Prose

David Bruce

Published by David Bruce, 2022.

This is a work of fiction. Similarities to real people, places, or events are entirely coincidental.

WILLIAM SHAKESPEARE'S CYMBELINE: A RETELLING IN PROSE

First edition. July 23, 2022.

ISBN: 979-8201401573

Written by David Bruce.

Table of Contents

Dedication

Dedicated to My Brother Frank

Frank was reluctant to write the words below, but he did at my request because it's an opportunity to show that people still do good deeds. This can help restore people's faith in humanity.

"I've put some thought into this, and here a few Good Deeds I've done.

"I've bought breakfast more than once for complete strangers at my favorite local diner (Tommy's Diner) just because they looked like they could use a free meal.

"A woman came into Tommy's Diner, looking like she could use a decent meal and would appreciate it being free. I watched as she walked through the restaurant and sat down. I thought to myself, 'Buy her lunch.' I fought the urge and told myself no. I looked at her after she ordered and received her meal and thought to myself, 'Buy her lunch.' Again, I told myself no. She is a complete stranger, and money is hard to come by for me as well as everyone else. I was in line at the check-out waiting to pay my bill. She came up and got into line behind me and I thought to myself, 'Buy her lunch!' I looked at her, she looked at me, I reached out and grabbed her ticket, but she didn't want to let go. I told her sort of sternly, 'I don't know why, but I really, really want to pay for your lunch. I know we are complete strangers, but I feel like I am supposed to pay for your lunch. Will you please give me the pleasure of paying for this?' She almost cried, but she did allow me the pleasure.

"In Columbus, Ohio, almost always someone is at the gas station wanting money. One day this guy asked for money. I asked him, 'Why do you want money?' He said he's hungry. (If you don't know, Speedway has hotdogs and other food and drink items.) I said, 'Come inside, I'll buy you something to eat.' He was a really nice guy. His name was Dave, and he was an Army veteran; he may have been a little mentally ill after serving in the military. He talked to me about the war (don't know what war) and how he was over there fighting bulldozers. I think a couple of hotdogs and a hot coffee made his day. It really put a smile on his face. I ended up liking this guy and I'd look for him when I was getting gas so I could help him out.

"One time a guy came in the restaurant selling an old leather jacket for $10.00 so he could get some gas. It didn't fit me, and I didn't want it anyway, but I bought it and then donated the jacket.

"A woman was driving her car with the alarm going off, so I helped her figure out how to turn it off. She had the key fob, so I'm sure she didn't steal the car.

"These are a few of the good deeds I've had the pleasure of doing."
***

The doing of good deeds is important. As a free person, you can choose to live your life as a good person or as a bad person. To be a good person, do good deeds. To be a bad person, do bad deeds. If you do good deeds, you will become good. If you do bad deeds, you will become bad. To become the person you want to be, act as if you already are that kind of person. Each of us chooses what kind of person we will become. To become a good person, do the things a good person does. To become a bad person, do the things a bad person does. The opportunity to take action to become the kind of person you want to be is yours.

Human beings have free will. According to the Babylonian Niddah 16b, whenever a baby is to be conceived, the Lailah (angel in charge of contraception) takes the drop of semen that will result in the conception and asks God, "Sovereign of the Universe, what is going to be the fate of this drop? Will it develop into a robust or into a weak person? An intelligent or a stupid person? A wealthy or a poor person?" The Lailah asks all these questions, but it does not ask, "Will it develop into a righteous or a wicked person?" The answer to that question lies in the decisions to be freely made by the human being that is the result of the conception.

A Buddhist monk visiting a class wrote this on the chalkboard: "EVERYONE WANTS TO SAVE THE WORLD, BUT NO ONE WANTS TO HELP MOM DO THE DISHES." The students laughed, but the monk then said, "Statistically, it's highly unlikely that any of you will ever have the opportunity to run into a burning orphanage and rescue an infant. But, in the smallest gesture of kindness — a warm smile, holding the door for the person behind you, shoveling the driveway of the elderly person next door — you have committed an act of immeasurable profundity, because to each of us, our life is our universe."

In her book titled I HAVE CHOSEN TO STAY AND FIGHT, comedian Margaret Cho writes, "I believe that we get complimentary snack-size portions of the afterlife, and we all receive them in a different way." For Ms. Cho, many of her snack-size portions of the afterlife come in hip hop music. Other people get different snack-size portions of the afterlife, and we all must be on the lookout for them when they come our way. And perhaps doing good deeds and experiencing good deeds are snack-size portions of the afterlife.

Educate Yourself
Read Like A Wolf Eats
Be Excellent to Each Other
Books Then, Books Now, Books Forever

***

In this retelling, as in all my retellings, I have tried to make the work of literature accessible to modern readers who may lack the knowledge about mythology, religion, and history that the literary work's contemporary audience had.

Do you know a language other than English? If you do, I give you permission to translate this book, copyright your translation, publish or self-publish it, and keep all the royalties for yourself. (Do give me credit, of course, for the original retelling.)

I would like to see my retellings of classic literature used in schools, so I give permission to the country of Finland (and all other countries) to give copies of this book to all students forever. I also give permission to the state of Texas (and all other states) to give copies of this book to all students forever. I also give permission to all teachers to give copies of this book to all students forever.

Teachers need not actually teach my retellings. Teachers are welcome to give students copies of my eBooks as background material. For example, if they are teaching Homer's *Iliad* and *Odyssey*, teachers are welcome to give students copies of my *Virgil's* Aeneid: *A Retelling in Prose* and tell students, "Here's another ancient epic you may want to read in your spare time

Cymbeline

Posthumus Leonatus, an orphan, has some problems. He married Imogen, a Princess, without the permission of her father, King Cymbeline of Britain. Because Posthumus was not born royalty and King Cymbeline does not want him to inherit the crown, Cymbeline banishes Posthumus, who goes to Italy. There he meets an Italian named Iachimo, who hears him boast about the faithfulness of his wife and who makes a bet with him. If Iachimo can seduce Imogen, then he will win a valuable diamond ring that she gave Posthumus, but if Iachimo cannot seduce Imogen, then he will give Posthumus many gold coins. The two men make the bet, and Iachimo goes to Britain to try to seduce Imogen.

CAST OF CHARACTERS

Male Characters

Cymbeline, King of Britain.

Cloten, son to the Queen by a former husband. The name "Cloten" rhymes with the word "rotten."

Posthumus Leonatus, a gentleman, husband to Imogen.

Belarius, a banished Lord, disguised under the name of Morgan.

Guiderius and Arviragus, sons to Cymbeline, supposed sons to Morgan; their names as Morgan's sons are Polydore and Cadwal. Guiderius (Polydore) is the older of the two. Guiderius and Arviragus are Welsh names.

Philario, friend to Posthumus.

Iachimo, friend to Philario.

A French Gentleman, friend to Philario.

Caius Lucius, general of the Roman forces, and an ambassador representing Caesar Augustus.

A Roman Captain.

Two British Captains.

Pisanio, servant to Posthumus, and to Imogen.

Cornelius, a physician.

Two Lords of Cymbeline's Court.

Two Gentlemen of the same.

Two Jailers.

Female Characters

Queen, wife to Cymbeline.

Imogen, daughter to Cymbeline by a former Queen.

Helen, a Lady attending on Imogen.

Miscellaneous Characters

Lords, Ladies, Roman Senators, Tribunes, a Dutch Gentleman, a Spanish Gentleman, a Soothsayer, Musicians, Officers, Captains, Soldiers, Messengers, and other Attendants, and Apparitions.

Scene: Sometimes in Britain, sometimes in Rome.

CHAPTER 1

— 1.1 —

Two gentlemen were speaking together in the garden of Cymbeline, King of Britain.

The first gantlemen said, "Every man you meet frowns. Just as the astrological planets influence our emotions, so the face of King Cymbeline influences the faces of our courtiers."

The second gentleman asked, "But what's the matter?"

"King Cymbeline's daughter, who is the heir of his Kingdom, and whom he intended to marry his wife's sole son — his wife is a widow whom he married — has given herself to a poor but worthy gentleman. She married him. Now her husband has been banished from the Kingdom, and she is imprisoned. Everyone has put on an appearance of outward sorrow, although I think the King is truly wounded to the center of his heart."

"None but the King has been wounded?"

"The man who has lost her is wounded, too; so is the Queen, who greatly desired the match. But none of the courtiers, although their faces bear the same grief-stricken look as the King's face bears, has a heart that is not glad at the thing they scowl at."

"Why is that?"

"The man who has lost the Princess is a thing too bad for a bad report, and he who has won her — I mean, the good man who has married her and has therefore been banished — is a creature such as, if you were to seek through the regions of the earth for another man who is his equal, there would be something lacking in whatever man you found and compared him to. I do not think that any other man has as fair an outward appearance and such a good character within as he does."

"You speak very highly of him."

"He is better than I have said he is. I am understating his good points and not fully revealing them."

"What's his name and family?"

The first gentleman said, "I cannot trace his family back very far. His father was named Sicilius; he fought with King Cassibelan against the Romans but he received his titles from King Tenantius, whom he served with glory and remarkable success and so gained the additional name Leonatus, which in Latin means "born from a lion." King Cassibelan was the great-uncle, and King Tenantius was the father, of King Cymbeline.

"Sicilius had, in addition to this gentleman who has married King Cymbeline's daughter, two other sons, who in the wars of the time died with their swords in hand. Because of this, Sicilius, their father, then old and fond of children, grieved so much that he died, and his gentle wife, who was then pregnant with this gentleman who has married King Cymbeline's daughter, died when he was born.

"King Cymbeline took the babe under his protection and named him Posthumus Leonatus. In our society, Posthumus is a common name for a baby born after the death of the father. King Cymbeline raised him and made him a member of his inner circle, and he made available to him all the education that was suitable for a person of his age. Posthumus received that education as we do air — as fast as it was ministered, and in his spring he became a harvest. He lived at court much praised and very loved — which is rare to do. He was an example to the youngest; to the more mature he was a mirror that served as a model of behavior to them; and to the older and graver he was a child who guided dotards. As for his wife, for marrying whom he is now banished, her own price proclaims how she esteemed him and his virtue — she was willing to marry him although it meant that she is now imprisoned. We can truly know what kind of man Posthumus is by knowing that such a worthy woman as Princess Imogen chose to marry him."

The second gentleman said, "I honor and admire Posthumus because of what you have told me about him. But please tell me, is Princess Imogen the sole child to King Cymbeline?"

"She is his only remaining child. He had two sons. If this is worth your hearing, take note of it. When the eldest of the two sons was three years old and the younger son was still in swaddling clothes, they were stolen from their nursery, and to this hour in all the fields of knowledge there is no credible guess which way they went."

"How long ago did this happen?"

"Some twenty years."

"It is difficult to believe that a King's children should be so slackly guarded, so kidnapped, and the search for them so slow and unable to trace them!"

"Although it is strange, and although the negligence involved may well be laughed at, yet it is true, sir."

"I entirely believe you."

"We must stop," the first gentleman said. "Here comes the gentleman Posthumus Leonatus, the Queen, and Princess Imogen."

The two gentlemen exited.

The Queen said to Imogen, "No, be assured you shall not find me, stepdaughter, despite the bad reputation of most stepmothers, evil-eyed toward you. You're my prisoner, but your jailer shall give you the keys that lock up your prison.

"As for you, Posthumus, as soon as I can win over the offended King, I will be your advocate; however, the fire of rage is still in him, and it would be good if you gave in to his sentence with whatever patience your wisdom may give to you."

"If it will please your highness," Posthumus said, "I will go away from here today."

"You know the danger," the Queen said. "I'll take a walk in the garden, pitying your pangs of barred affections, and allow you two to be together, although the King has ordered that you two should not speak together."

The Queen exited.

Imogen, who disliked the Queen, said, "Oh, hypocritical kindness and courtesy! How well this tyrant can tickle where she wounds! My dearest husband, I somewhat fear my father's wrath, but although I will always honor my father, I do not fear what his rage can do to me. You must go into exile, and I shall here endure the continual glances of angry eyes. I will not enjoy the comforts of life, except that I know I may see again a jewel — you — who is in the world."

Posthumus said to Imogen, "My Queen! My wife! Oh, lady, weep no more, lest I give cause to be suspected of crying and feeling more tender emotions than is suitable for a man. I will remain the most loyal husband who has ever made marriage vows. I will reside in Rome with a man named Philario who was a friend to my father, and to me is known only by letter. Write there to me, my

Queen, and with my eyes I'll drink the words you send, even if the ink with which they are written is made of gall."

Gall, which was then used in making ink, is a bitter substance that oak trees exude.

The Queen returned and said, "Be quick, please. If the King comes here and sees you two together, I shall incur I don't know how much of his displeasure."

She thought, *Yet I'll persuade him to walk this way. I never do him wrong without him enduring my injuries in order to be friends with me. He pays dearly for my offences.*

The Queen exited.

Posthumus said, "Even if we were to take as long to say goodbye as we have years left to live, the loathness to separate would grow. *Adieu*!"

"No, stay a little longer," Imogen said. "If you were going to ride on horseback a while to get some fresh air, this kind of goodbye would be too little. Look here, love; this diamond ring belonged to my mother. Take it, sweetheart; keep it until you woo another wife, after I, Imogen, am dead."

"What!" Posthumus said. "Another wife? You gentle gods, give me only this wife I have, and wrap up in a shroud any embracings for a new wife. Instead of a new wife, give me death!"

He put Imogen's ring on his finger and said to it, "Remain here while sense can keep it on."

Posthumus intended to wear the ring for the rest of his life.

He then said to Imogen, "And, sweetest, fairest, just as I my poor self did exchange for you, to your so infinite loss, so in our gifts I still get the better of you. You are a better person than I am, and your gift to me is better than my gift to you. For my sake, wear this; it is a manacle of love. I'll place it upon this fairest prisoner."

He put a bracelet on her arm.

Imogen said, "Oh, the gods! When shall we see each other again?"

King Cymbeline and some lords entered the garden.

"The King!" Posthumus said.

Seeing him, Cymbeline said, "You basest thing, leave! Go away, and get out of my sight! If after this command you burden the court with your unworthiness, you die! Go away! You are poison to my blood."

"May the gods protect you!" Posthumus said. "And may they bless the good people who remain in the court! I am leaving."

He exited.

Imogen said, "There cannot be a pain, even in dying, sharper than this pain is."

Cymbeline said to her, "Oh, disloyal thing, you should make me feel younger, but instead you have heaped an age of years on me."

"I beg you, sir, do not harm yourself with your vexation," Imogen replied. "I am oblivious to your wrath; a pain more exquisite than your wrath subdues all my pains, all my fears."

"Are you past grace? Past obedience?" Cymbeline asked.

Cymbeline used the word "grace" to mean "sense of propriety or sense of duty."

"I am past hope, and I am in despair," Imogen said. "In that way, I am past grace."

Imogen used the word "grace" to mean "mercy or forgiveness." According to Christianity, a person who is in despair and feels that God cannot forgive him or her will not repent and so will be condemned to spend eternity in Hell. Such a person commits a sin of pride by believing that he or she has committed a sin so great that God cannot forgive it; God is great and merciful and can and will forgive any sin as long as it is sincerely repented. Imogen, however, was despairing because she and her husband were separated.

"You could have married the sole son of my Queen!"

"I am blest that I did not!" Imogen replied. "I chose an eagle, and I avoided choosing an ignoble, greedy, grasping puttock — a kite, a bird of prey."

"You married a beggar; you would have made my throne a seat for baseness."

"No; instead, I added a luster to your throne."

"Oh, you vile person!"

"Sir, it is your fault that I have loved Posthumus. You raised him as my playfellow, and he is a man who is worth any woman. The sum he paid for marrying me — exile — is almost more than I am worth."

"Are you mad?" Cymbeline asked.

"I am almost insane, sir. May Heaven restore me! I wish I were the daughter of a cowherd, and my Posthumus Leonatus were the son of our neighbor the shepherd! Then we could be married without any problems."

"You foolish thing!"

The Queen returned, and using the royal plural King Cymbeline said, "Posthumus and Imogen were together again. You have disobeyed our command."

He then ordered his attendants, "Away with Imogen, and pen her up."

"I beg you to be calm, Cymbeline," the Queen said. "Peace, dear lady stepdaughter, peace! Sweet sovereign, leave us for a while. Think about this matter for a while, and you will feel much better."

"No, let her languish and lose a drop of blood a day; and, when she is old, let her die from this folly!" Cymbeline said.

In this society, people believed that they lost a drop of blood each time they sighed. Cymbeline wanted his daughter to grieve and feel ill until she got old and died.

King Cymbeline and his lords exited.

The Queen said to him as he left, "Bah! You must give way. You must give in."

Pisanio, a servant to Imogen and Posthumus, entered the garden.

The Queen said to Imogen, "Here is your servant."

Then the Queen asked Pisanio, "How are you, sir! What news do you have?"

"My lord your son drew on my master. Your son drew his sword against my master, Posthumus."

"No harm, I trust, is done?"

"There might have been, except that my master played rather than fought — he kept calm and was not angry," Pisanio said. "They were parted by some gentlemen who were at hand."

"I am very glad of it," the Queen said.

Imogen said to the Queen, "Your son is the friend of my father; he takes his part."

She added sarcastically, "He drew his sword upon an exile! Oh, what a brave sir! I wish they were both together in Africa and I was nearby with a needle so that I might prick whoever tried to withdraw from their fight."

She then said to Pisanio, "Why have you come here from your master?"

"He commanded me to come here," Pisanio replied. "He would not allow me to accompany him to the harbor."

Pisanio handed Imogen a paper and said, "He left these notes concerning what commands I should be subject to when it pleased you to employ me."

The Queen said to Imogen, "This man has been your faithful servant. I dare to bet my honor that he will remain your faithful servant."

"I humbly thank your highness," Pisanio said to the Queen.

"Please, let us walk awhile," the Queen said to Imogen.

Imogen said to Pisanio, "About a half-hour from now, please come and talk with me. You shall at least go help my husband get onboard his ship. Leave me and do that."

The Queen's son, Cloten, talked in a public place with two lords shortly after his fight with Posthumus.

The first lord said to Cloten, "Sir, I would advise you to change your shirt; the violence of action has made you reek — that is, steam — like a burnt sacrifice."

Because the first lord was a flatterer, he added, "Where air comes out, air comes in. No air outside is as wholesome as the air you vent."

Cloten replied, "If my shirt were bloody, then I would change it. Have I hurt Posthumus?"

The second lord thought, *No, truly; you have not hurt even his patience.*

"Hurt him!" the first lord said. "His body's a passable and navigable carcass, if he is not hurt: It is a thoroughfare for steel, if it is not hurt. If you have not hurt him, then his body has hidden cavities into which you thrust your sword!"

The second lord thought, *Cloten's steel sword was in debt; like a debtor, it avoided the creditor — Posthumus — and traveled the side streets rather going downtown.*

"The villain would not make a stand against me," Cloten said. "He would not hold his ground."

The second lord thought, *Posthumus fled, all right — he constantly fled forward, toward your face.*

The first lord said, "Make a stand against you! Hold his ground! You have land enough of your own, but he added to your having; he gave you some ground."

The second lord thought, *Posthumus gave Cloten as many inches of ground as Cloten has oceans — none!*

He then thought about Cloten and the first lord, *Young pups!*

Cloten said, "I wish the bystanders had not come between Posthumus and me."

The second lord thought, *I wish that they had not come between you two until you had fallen and measured upon the ground how long a fool you are.*

Cloten complained, "And that she should love this fellow — Posthumus — and refuse me!"

The second lord thought, *If it is a sin to make a truly worthy choice of a man to be her husband, then she is damned.*

The first lord said, "Sir, as I have always told you, her beauty and her brain do not go together. She's a pretty woman, but I have seen little evidence of any intelligence she might have. I have seen small reflection of her wit."

The second lord thought, *She shines not upon fools, lest the reflection of her shine should hurt her.*

Cloten said, "Come, I'll go to my chamber. I wish there had been some hurt done!"

The second lord thought, *I don't wish that there had been some hurt done, unless it had been the fall of an ass, which is no great hurt.*

Noticing the second lord for the first time, Cloten asked him, "You'll go with us?"

An uncomfortable silence followed — the second lord did not like Cloten's company. To stop the silence, the first lord said, "I'll go with your lordship."

Cloten said to the second lord, "Come, let's go together."

As son to the Queen, Cloten was a powerful person, so the second lord said, "Very well, my lord."

Imogen and Pisanio spoke together in a room in King Cymbeline's palace.

Imogen said to Pisanio, "I wish you would cling to the shores of the harbor, and question sailors on every ship. If Posthumus should write me a letter and I not receive it, it would be a paper lost — a loss as serious as the loss of a pardon. What was the last thing that he said to you?"

Pisanio replied, "He spoke about you: 'My Queen! My Queen!'"

"Did he then wave his handkerchief?"

"Yes, and he kissed it, madam."

"Linen that was unaware of the kiss! And yet the linen was more fortunate than I am because it was kissed! And was that all?"

"No, madam; as long as he could make me with my eyes or ears distinguish him from the others onboard ship, he stayed on the deck and kept waving his glove, or hat, or handkerchief. It was like he was expressing the fits and stirs of his mind — his soul all so slowly sailed away from you, no matter how swiftly his ship sailed."

Imogen said, "You should have stayed and watched him until he was as small as a crow, or smaller, before you left. You should have gazed after him that long."

"Madam, I did."

"I would have broken my eyes and cracked them," Imogen said. "I would have looked as long as I could look upon him, until the distance between us had made him the size of the sharp end of my needle. No, my eyes would have followed him until he had melted from the smallness of a gnat to invisible air, and then I would have turned my eyes away and wept. But, good Pisanio, when shall we hear from him?"

"Be assured, madam, he shall write you at the first opportunity."

"I did not take my proper leave of him," Imogen said. "I had very pretty things to say to him, but before I could tell him how I would think certain thoughts about him at certain hours, and before I could make him swear that the women of Italy should not betray my interest and his honor, and before I was able to make him promise to pray at the same time as me — at the sixth hour of the morning, at noon, and at midnight — for then my solicitations on his behalf would be in Heaven, and before I could give him that parting kiss that I had set between two enchanting words to protect him from evil, my father came in and like the tyrannous breathing and blowing of the north wind, he shook all our buds of love and kept them from growing."

A lady entered the room and said to Imogen, "The Queen, madam, desires your highness' company."

Imogen said to Pisanio, "Those things I told you to do, get them done. I will attend the Queen."

"Madam, I shall," Pisanio replied.

In a room in Philario's house in Italy, a number of people were speaking about Posthumus. They were Philario, Iachimo, and a Frenchman, a Dutchman, and a Spaniard. Iachimo and the others were friends of Philario's.

Iachimo said, "Believe it, sir, I have seen Posthumus in Britain. He was then of growing reputation, expected to prove as worthy as since he has been so called, but I could then have looked on him without the help of wonder and amazement, even if the catalog of his endowments had been written on a tablet by his side and I was able to peruse him with the benefit of the items written in the catalog. He was not all that impressive."

Philario replied, "You are talking about him when he was less furnished than he is now with that which makes him distinguished both without and within. Now, he is more distinguished than he was then, both in his appearance and in his character."

The Frenchman said, "I have seen Posthumus in France. We had very many men there who could behold the Sun with as firm eyes as he."

The Frenchman was referring to the eagle, a symbol of nobility, which was reputed to be able to look at the Sun without blinking. Like Iachimo, the Frenchman was wondering if Posthumus' excellent reputation was inflated.

Iachimo said, "This matter of marrying his King's daughter, wherein he must be weighed rather by her value than by his own, has given him an excellent reputation that I am sure he does not deserve."

The Frenchman said, "His banishment also plays a role in his reputation."

"That is true," Iachimo said. "Many who mourn the lamentable separation of Posthumus Leonatus and Princess Imogen and who are on the side of the Princess have given their approval of Posthumus, and this has greatly boosted his reputation and has served to justify her choice of him as husband. If not for that, a case might easily be made that she made the wrong choice when she took as her husband a beggar — which I say Posthumus is without even taking into account his lower rank. But how is it that he comes here to stay with you, Philario? How did he creep into your life and become acquainted with you?"

Philario replied, "His father and I were soldiers together; to his father I have been often bound for no less than my life. On more than one occasion, he saved my life."

He heard a noise, looked up and saw Posthumus coming toward them, and said, "Here comes the Briton. Let him be so entertained among you as gentlemen of your savoir-faire should treat a stranger of his quality and rank. Treat him well. I beg all of you to become acquainted with this gentleman, whom I commend to you as a noble friend of mine. How worthy he is I will leave to appear hereafter, rather than to tell you his story and accomplishments in his own hearing."

The Frenchman said to Posthumus, "Sir, we have met in Orleans."

Posthumus replied, "Since that time I have been debtor to you for courtesies that I will never be able to pay for in full."

"Sir, you overrate my poor kindness," the Frenchman said. "I was glad I was able to reconcile my countryman and you. It would have been a pity if you two should have fought a deadly duel about so slight and trivial a matter."

"I beg your pardon, sir," Posthumus said. "I was then a young and inexperienced traveller; I did not always agree with what I heard because I did not want my every action to be guided by others' experiences. But upon my improved judgment — I hope that I do not offend anyone if I say that my judgment has improved — my quarrel was not altogether slight."

"I disagree," the Frenchman said. "The quarrel was to be decided by a duel fought by two people, one of whom would in all likelihood have destroyed the other, or perhaps both of you would have fallen."

Iachimo asked, "Can we, without causing offense, ask what the quarrel was about?"

"You can, I think," the Frenchman said. "It was a quarrel in public, which I may tell you about without anyone contradicting me. It was much like the argument that fell out between us last night, where each of us began to praise our country's women. This gentleman — Posthumus — at that time was vouching — and pledging that he would bloodily fight anyone who disagreed — that his lady was more beautiful, virtuous, wise, chaste, constant and true, and less capable of being seduced than any of the rarest of our ladies in France."

Iachimo said, "That lady is not now living, or this gentleman's opinion has changed by this time."

Posthumus replied, "She is still alive and still virtuous, and I have not changed my opinion."

Iachimo said, "You must not so far esteem her above our ladies of Italy."

Posthumus said, "Even if I were as provoked as I was in France, I would not lessen my opinion of her, though I profess myself her adorer, not her lover. To me, she is more than a piece of flesh."

"As beautiful and as good — a kind of hand-in-hand comparison; in other words, saying that British ladies and Italian ladies were equals — would have been an opinion too fair and too good for any lady in Britain," Iachimo said. "If your lady goes before others I have seen, as that diamond ring of yours outshines many I have seen, I could not but believe that she excelled many ladies, but I have not seen the most precious diamond ring that exists, nor have you seen the most precious lady who exists."

"I praised her as I rated her," Posthumus said. "I do the same thing with my diamond ring."

"What do you esteem it at?" Iachimo said. "What do you value it at?"

"I value it at more than the world possesses."

"Either your unparagoned — unequalled — mistress is dead, or she's outprized by a ring," Iachimo said. "The lady is part of the world, so the diamond ring is more valuable than she is."

Posthumus replied, "You are mistaken. The diamond ring may be sold, or given, if there were wealth enough for the purchase, or merit for the gift. The lady is not a thing for sale, and only the gods can give such a gift."

"Is she a gift whom the gods have given you?" Iachimo asked.

"The lady is my wife: Princess Imogen. I will keep her, by the graces of the gods."

"You have married her, and you may wear — enjoy — her because she is legally yours," Iachimo said, "but, you know, strange fowl light upon neighboring ponds."

In this society, the word "pond" was slang for "vagina."

Iachimo continued, "Your ring may be stolen, too. Of your brace — your duo — of treasures beyond price, the lady is frail and the diamond ring is subject to accident and chance. A cunning thief or a that-way-accomplished courtier would run risks to win both."

Posthumus said, "Your Italy does not contain a courtier accomplished enough to overcome the honor of my wife, if you think her frail in the holding or the loss of her honor. I don't doubt that Italy has an abundance of thieves; notwithstanding, I'm not afraid I will lose my ring."

"Let's stop this conversation, gentlemen," Philario said. "Let's change the subject and talk about something else."

"Sir, with all my heart," Posthumus said. "This worthy signior, I thank him, does not consider me a stranger; we are familiar — not formal — with each other right from the start."

"With five times as much conversation," Iachimo said, "I could get ground on your fair mistress, I could make her retreat, and I could even make her yield to me, if I had admittance into her company and the opportunity to befriend and become acquainted with her."

"No, no," Posthumus said.

"I dare to bet half of my estate against your ring," Iachimo said. "In my opinion, half of my estate somewhat exceeds your ring in value, but I make my wager rather against your confidence in your wife than against her reputation, and to stop your giving offence with your confidence, I dare to attempt to seduce any lady in the world."

Iachimo's words are interesting. A close examination of his words reveals that he is betting that he can shake Posthumus' confidence in the chastity of his wife. Chastity means refraining from unlawful sexual intercourse; a chaste woman can have lawful sex with her husband, but she will not engage in adultery. One of the ways for Iachimo to shake Posthumus' confidence in the chastity of his wife would be for Iachimo to seduce her, but there are other ways for him to shake Posthumus' confidence in the chastity of his wife.

Posthumus replied, "You are a great deal deceived in holding this very bold opinion of women, and I don't doubt that you will receive what you deserve if you dare to attempt to accomplish what you say you will do."

"What's that?" Iachimo asked.

"You will deserve a repulse, though your 'attempt,' as you call it, deserves more; it deserves a punishment, too."

Philario attempted to make peace between the two men: "Gentlemen, enough of this. This argument was born too suddenly; let it die as it was born, and, please, become better acquainted and friends with each other."

"I wish that I had bet my estate *and* my neighbor's that I can do what I have spoken about!" Iachimo said.

"What lady would you choose to assail and seduce?" Posthumus asked.

"Yours," Iachimo replied, "your wife who in constancy and faithfulness to you, you think stands so safe. I will bet you ten thousand ducats against your ring that if you write me a letter of introduction to the court where your lady is and give me no more advantage than the opportunity of a second meeting with your wife, I will bring from thence that honor of hers that you imagine so preserved. If I can meet her only twice, I can seduce her."

"I will wage against your gold the same amount of gold, but I will not bet my ring," Posthumus replied. "My ring I value as dearly as I do my finger; it is part of it."

"You are afraid to bet your ring, and therein you are the wiser. You know your wife well, and you know what you can afford to bet on her. Even if you buy ladies' flesh at a million units of money for one dram — an exorbitant price — you cannot preserve it from being tainted. I see that you have some religion in you because you fear. My bet has put the fear of God in you. You are afraid that your lady will sin, and you are afraid that you will lose the bet."

"This is only macho talk of the kind that you are accustomed to speak," Posthumus said. "You have something more serious in mind, I hope."

"I am the master of my speech, and I will undertake to do what I have said that I will do," Iachimo said. "I swear it."

"Will you? I shall give my diamond ring to Philario to hold until your return," Posthumus said. "It shall be only a loan — I will get it back. Let there be a legal agreement drawn up between us concerning this bet. My wife exceeds in goodness the hugeness of your unworthy thinking. I dare you to compete against her."

He then offered his ring to Philario, saying, "Here's my ring."

"I will not allow this bet," Philario said, declining to take the ring.

"By the gods, the bet is already made," Iachimo said.

He then said to Posthumus, "If I bring you no sufficient testimony that I have enjoyed the dearest bodily part of your wife, my ten thousand ducats are yours, and your diamond ring, too. If I leave the court and give up my efforts and leave her with such honor as you trust she has, she your jewel, this your jewel, and my gold are yours — provided I have your letter of introduction so that I may be well received at the court and am able to have a conversation with your wife."

"I agree to these conditions," Posthumus said. "Let us have a legal agreement drawn up between us. However, let us add these conditions. If you make your attempt to seduce my wife and give me direct evidence that you have prevailed, I am no further your enemy; if she can be seduced, she is not worth our being enemies. However, if she remains unseduced, and you are not able to make it appear otherwise, then for your ill opinion of her and the assault you have made against her chastity, you shall answer me with your sword — we shall fight a duel."

Posthumus' words are interesting: "if she remains unseduced, *and* you are not able to make it appear otherwise ...." Part of the bet was that Iachimo would not be able to convince Posthumus that his wife had committed adultery. Of course, it is possible that Iachimo could fail to seduce Posthumus' wife and yet convince Posthumus that he — Iachimo — had succeeded in seducing Posthumus' wife.

"Give me your hand," Iachimo said. "Let us make a contract between us. We will have these things set down by lawful counsel, and I will leave immediately for Britain, lest our agreement catch cold and starve and die. I will fetch my gold ducats and we will have our two wagers recorded. Someone will hold on to my gold ducats and your ring until we know which of us has won our wager."

The two wagers were the stakes that each was putting up. The loser of the bet would lose his wager.

Posthumus said, "I agree."

Posthumus and Iachimo exited.

The Frenchman asked Philario, "Will they really do this, do you think?"

"Signior Iachimo will not back down from it," Philario replied. "Come, let us follow them."

In a room in King Cymbeline's palace in Britain, the Queen and Doctor Cornelius, who made medicines and poisons from plants, were speaking. Some ladies attended the Queen.

The Queen said, "While the dew is still on the ground, gather those flowers. Be quick. Who has the list of the flowers I need?"

The first lady said, "I do, madam."

"Go, and hurry," the Queen said.

The ladies exited to gather the flowers.

The Queen said, "Now, master doctor, have you brought those drugs?"

"If it pleases your highness, yes, I have," Doctor Cornelius replied. "Here they are, madam."

He gave her a small box and said, "But I beg your grace, without meaning to offend you — my conscience makes me ask you this — why have you commanded me to bring you these most poisonous compounds, which are the causers of a languishing death? Though those compounds work slowly, they are deadly."

"I wonder, doctor, why you ask me such a question," the Queen said. "Haven't I been your pupil for a long time? Haven't you taught me how to make perfumes? How to distil? How to preserve? Yes, I have been. Our great King himself often asks me for my confections. Having thus far proceeded — unless you think me devilish and engaging in black magic — isn't it suitable for me to increase my knowledge in areas related to what I already know? I will try the effects of these your compounds on such creatures as we count not worth the hanging, but on no human. I will test the compounds' vigor and apply antidotes to their poison, and by these experiments I will learn the compounds' several virtues and effects."

Doctor Cornelius replied, "Your highness shall from these experiments only make your heart hard. Besides, seeing these effects will be both harmful and infectious. Handling such poisons is dangerous."

"Oh, settle down," the Queen said. "Be calm."

Pisanio, the servant of Posthumus Leonatus and Princess Imogen, entered the room.

The Queen thought, *Here comes a flattering rascal. Upon him I will first work. He's loyal to his master, and he is an enemy to my son.*

She asked, "How are you now, Pisanio?"

She then said to Cornelius, "Doctor, your service for this time is ended. Go on your way."

Doctor Cornelius thought, *I suspect you, madam, but you shall do no harm.*

Rather than leaving immediately, he watched the Queen interact with Pisanio. He also kept an eye on the box of compounds she was holding.

The Queen said to Pisanio, "Listen, I want to have a word with you."

They talked quietly.

Doctor Cornelius thought, *I do not like her. She thinks she has a box of strange, unnatural, slow-acting poisons. I know her spirit, and I will not trust one of her malice with a poison of such damned nature. Those compounds she has will stupefy and dull the senses for a while. First, probably, she'll test them on cats and dogs, and then afterwards on higher animals, but there is no danger in the show of death the compounds cause. All that will happen is that the spirit will be locked up for a while and then will revive, refreshed. She will be fooled by a very false and deceptive effect, and I will be all the truer the more I am false to her. By lying to her, I will be a better person.*

Noticing that Doctor Cornelius was still present, the Queen said to him, "No further service is needed, doctor, until I send for you."

He replied, "I humbly take my leave," and then he exited.

The Queen said to Pisanio, "She still weeps, you say? Don't you think that in time she will stop crying and follow advice while rejecting the folly she now possesses? Work on her. When you bring me word that she loves my son, I'll tell you immediately that you are as great as is your master — no, greater, because all his fortunes lie speechless as if they were on a deathbed and his name is at its last gasp. He cannot return to our court, nor can he continue to remain where he is. To shift his place of residence is just to exchange one misery for another, and every day that comes to him is simply another day wasted. What shall you expect if you are dependent on a thing who leans and needs support, who cannot be newly built, and who has no friends, not even as many as are needed to prop him up?"

The Queen dropped the box of compounds, and Pisanio picked it up for her.

The Queen said to him, "You have picked up you know not what, but take it for your labor. It is a thing that I made, which has saved the King's life five times. I do not know anything that has better medicinal value. Please, take it; it is a down payment on the further good things that I mean to do for you. Tell the mistress you serve, Princess Imogene, how the case stands with her. Tell her to love my son, and tell her that as if it came from your heart. Think what an opportunity this is to change and improve your life. You will still serve Princess Imogen, but in addition my son will take notice of you. I'll persuade King Cymbeline to give you anything you desire, and I, who have set on you this course of action that shall give you good things, will chiefly and richly reward you for persuading Princess Imogen to love my son. Call my female servants to come to me. Most importantly, think about my words."

Pisanio exited to get the female servants to come to the Queen.

The Queen thought about Pisanio, *He is a sly and loyal knave. He is not one to be diverted from doing his duty to Posthumus Leonatus and to Princess Imogen. He acts as Posthumus' agent at the court, and he is a constant reminder to Princess Imogen to remain loyal to her marriage vows. I have given him compounds that, if he takes them, shall quite remove from Princess Imogen this chief advocate for her sweetheart. After Pisanio dies of poison, Princess Imogen — unless she changes her mind and loves my son — shall taste the poison, too.*

Pisanio returned with the Queen's attendants.

The Queen said to the attendants, who were carrying the flowers they had gathered, "Good, good. Well done, well done. Take the violets, cowslips, and primroses to my private room."

She added, "Fare you well, Pisanio. Think about my words."

The Queen and her dependents exited.

Alone, Pisanio said to himself, "And I shall do so. But when to my good lord I prove untrue, I'll choke myself. That is all I'll do for you."

In another room of the palace, Princess Imogen sat alone.

She said to herself, "A cruel father, and a treacherous stepmother, a foolish suitor to a wedded lady whose husband has been banished — the banishment of my husband is my supreme crown of grief! These are my vexations, and I endure them day after day. If I had been kidnapped as my two brothers were, then I would have been happy because I could have married without problems the man I chose. Most miserable are those who have an unfulfilled longing for glorious things; blessed are those, however humble and impoverished, who have gotten their humble and honest desires, thereby giving a relish to their comfort."

She saw Pisanio and a strange man — Iachimo — coming toward her, and said to herself, "Who may this man be? Bah!"

Pisanio said to her, "Madam, this is a noble gentleman of Rome, who has come from my lord, Posthumus, with a letter."

Iachimo, seeing Princess Imogen looking sad, said to her, "Cheer up, madam. I bring good news. The worthy Posthumus Leonatus is safe and he dearly and deeply greets your highness."

He gave her a letter from Posthumus.

Imogen replied, "Thanks, good sir. You're kindly welcome."

Iachimo thought, *All of her that is on the outside is very rich! She is beautiful! If she has a mind that matches her rare beauty, she is alone the Arabian bird, and I have lost the wager.*

The Arabian bird is the mythological Phoenix, of which only one exists at a time. When old, the Phoenix burns itself and is reconstituted from the ashes. Iachimo, whose opinion of women was poor, believed that Imogen, if she had a mind that matched her beauty, was as rare as the Phoenix — she was the only chaste woman on the planet.

Iachimo thought, *May boldness be my friend! Arm me, audacity, from head to foot! Or, like the Parthian, I shall fight while fleeing. Or else I shall give up trying to win the wager and shall directly flee.*

The Parthians fought on horseback. They would charge their horses at the enemy and throw their spears, and then shoot arrows while riding back to their ranks. Iachimo was praying for the boldness to directly attempt to seduce Imogen. The alternatives were to be indirect and convince Posthumus that he — Iachimo — had seduced Imogen, although he had not, or to give up trying to win the wager.

Imogen read part of the letter out loud, the part that praised Iachimo: *"He is one of the noblest reputation and distinction, to whose kindnesses I am most infinitely tied. Welcome him accordingly, as you value your trust — LEONATUS."*

She then said, "So far I read aloud, but not the rest. But even the very middle of my heart is warmed by the rest, and takes it thankfully. You are as welcome, worthy sir, as I have words to bid you, and you shall find that you are welcome in all that I can do for you."

"Thanks, fairest lady," Iachimo said.

He then began his attempt to seduce Imogen by pretending to have distracting thoughts. He pretended to be wondering how Posthumus could be unfaithful to a woman such as Imogen. In doing so, he spoke disjointedly and not clearly.

He said, as if to himself but making sure that Imogen could hear him, "What, are men mad? Has nature given them eyes to see this vaulted arch, and the rich harvest of sea and land, which can distinguish between the fiery orbs above and the twinned stones upon the numbered beach? And can we not make division with spectacles so precious between fair and foul?"

Iachimo was saying, in unclear language, that he could not believe that Posthumus was unable to recognize the worth of Imogen. Men are able to see the sky, the sea, and the land, and they know the difference between the Sun and the Moon and the differences among the grains of sand of the beach — grains that look alike and are so numerous that only God can count them. On the Earth we see sights and can tell them one from another and tell which sight is more spectacular and better than the others. Why then can't men — and especially Posthumus — tell the difference between fair and foul, between Imogen and other women?

Imogen asked him, "What is causing your amazement?"

Iachimo continued, "The faulty perception cannot be in the eye, because apes and monkeys between two such females would chatter approvingly toward the better female and contemn with grimaces the other female. Nor can the faulty perception lie in the judgment because idiots in this case of favor would be wisely definite — in such a case even fools would definitely make the wise choice and realize which is the best woman. Nor can the faulty perception lie in the sexual appetite. Sluttishness opposed to such elegant excellence would make sexual desire turn into dry heaves and not be tempted to feed."

"What is the matter, I wonder?" Imogen said.

Iachimo said, "The overfilled sexual desire, which has been satiated and is yet unsatisfied, which is a tub that has been filled and is yet leaking, which has feasted first on the lamb and is yet longing to feast on garbage ...."

The lamb is a symbol of purity. Iachimo was hinting — make that lying — that Posthumus had enjoyed sex with Imogen but yet was pursuing sex with garbage, aka whores.

Imogen asked, "What, dear sir, is making you rapt? Are you well?"

"Thank you, madam," Iachimo replied. "I am well."

To get Pisanio out of the way, Iachimo said to him, "I beg you, sir, to tell my servant to wait for me where I left him. My servant is a foreigner here, and he is a worrier. He may be wondering about what he should do."

"I was going, sir," Pisanio said, "to welcome him."

Pisanio exited to carry out his errand.

"Is my husband well?" Imogen asked Iachimo. "Please tell me whether he is healthy."

"He is well, madam."

"Is he disposed to be mirthful? I hope he is."

"He is very cheerful. None of the other foreigners there is as merry and playful. He is called the British reveler."

"When he was here," Imogen said, "he was inclined to be solemn and often he did not know why."

"I have never seen him solemn," Iachimo said. "There is a Frenchman who is his companion, a person who is an eminent monsieur who, it seems, loves very much a French girl at home. The Frenchman sends out like a furnace very many warm sighs, while the jolly Brit — your husband, I mean — laughs from his open and unimpeded lungs and cries, 'Oh, can my sides hold, when I think that a man, who knows by history, report, or his own experience what women are, yes, what she cannot choose but must be, will during his free hours languish for assured and betrothed bondage?'"

"Does my husband say that?" Imogen asked.

"Yes, madam, with his eyes drowned in a flood of tears with laughter. It is entertaining to be nearby and hear him mock the Frenchman. But, Heavens know, some men are much to blame."

"Not my husband, I hope."

"Not he," Iachimo said, "but yet Heaven's bounty towards him might be used more thankfully. In himself, Heaven has given him many gifts; Heaven has also given him you, whom I judge to be more valuable than all his other gifts. While I am bound to wonder at these gifts, I am bound to pity, too."

"What do you pity, sir?"

"I heartily pity two creatures," Iachimo replied, looking at Imogen.

He was pretending that he pitied Posthumus and Imogen.

"Am I one of the creatures you pity, sir?" Imogen asked. "You are looking at me. What fault do you see in me that deserves your pity?"

"This is lamentable! Should I hide myself from the radiant Sun and find solace in the dungeon by the smoldering burnt-out wick of a candle?"

Imogene was speaking deliberately unclearly, but he was saying that he was attracted to Imogen and the difference between her and any other woman was the difference between the Sun and the burning stub of a candle that was about to go out.

"Please, sir," Imogen said, "speak more clearly when you answer my questions. Why do you pity me?"

"That others do — I was about to say — enjoy your — but it is the duty of the gods to avenge it, not mine to speak about it."

Iachimo was lying that the gods needed to avenge what Posthumus was doing to his marriage — Iachimo was lying that other women were enjoying Imogen's husband.

"You seem to know something about me, or something that concerns me," Imogen said. "Please — since thinking that things may be ill often hurts more than being sure that they are because certain knowledge means knowing that things cannot be remedied, or if the ill things are known in time, the way to remedy them is also known — tell me what you start to say and then stop saying."

Iachimo said, "Suppose I had this cheek to bathe my lips upon. Suppose I had this hand, whose touch, whose every touch, would force the feeler's soul to take an oath of loyalty. Suppose I had this object, which takes prisoner the wild motions of my eyes, fixing it only here."

"This object" referred to Imogen; he was objectifying her.

Iachimo continued, "If I had all this, then would I, who would be damned if I should do these things, sloppily kiss lips as common as the stairs that everyone climbs to the Capitol in Rome; clasp hands made hard by telling lies each hour, hands made as hard by lying as by laboring; and then glance sideways into eyes as base and ill-lustrous as the smoky light that is fed with stinking tallow? If I would do these things, then it would be fitting that all the plagues of Hell should at the same time come to the one who revolts."

Iachimo was lying that Posthumus was revolting against the vows of marriage.

Again, his language was unclear. What does it mean to say that hands are made hard by lying? A person who works hard will have hard hands. Prostitutes can work hard, but their work involves a kind of lying. Married people make a legal contract that allows them to have sex, but prostitutes have sex without having first made the legal contract; prostitutes act as if they are married, but they are not married — at least, not to their customers. Acting as if they are married although they are not married is a kind of lie. Iachimo was also saying that the prostitutes with whom Posthumus was having sex were hardworking — they slept with many, many men. If they were to work in the fields rather than in bed, they would have hard hands indeed. Metaphorically, the hands of prostitutes are hard.

"My lord, I fear, has forgotten Britain," Imogen replied.

"And himself," Iachimo said. "I am not inclined to tell you this information regarding your husband's change and descent into baseness, but your virtues charm this information from my most silent inmost thought and bring it to my tongue."

"Let me hear no more," Imogen said. "Tell me no more."

"Oh, dearest soul!" Iachimo said. "Your situation strikes my heart with pity so much that it makes me sick. A lady as beautiful as you, the heir to an empire, would make the greatest King double in happiness and success. And yet you share your husband with prostitutes who are paid with money that you give to him. You share your husband with diseased whores who have sex with everyone for gold, despite their many infirmities that rottenness gives to a human being!

Such stuff — whores — who 'boil' in vats filled with hot water used to treat venereal disease is enough to be poisonous to poison! Be revenged on your husband, or she who gave birth to you was no Queen, and you fall away from and make degenerate your great stock."

"Be revenged on my husband!" Imogen said. "How should I be revenged? If this is true — my heart will not easily allow my ears to abuse it — if what you say is true, how should I be revenged?"

Iachimo replied, "Should he make me live, like Diana's virginal priests, between cold sheets, while he is vaulting variable ramps — jumping on various whores — in contemptuous disregard of you, paying the whores with your money?"

Although Iachimo used the word "me," referring to himself, he meant his words to apply to Imogen — why should she live without sex while her husband is having lots of sex with other women?

Iachimo continued, "Get revenge. I dedicate myself to your sweet pleasure. I am nobler than that runaway from your bed, and I will remain steadfast to your affection. I will be secretive about what we do as well as loyal to you."

"Pisanio!" Imogen called. "Come here!"

"Let me offer you my service by kissing your lips," Iachimo said.

"Get away from me!" Imogen said. "I condemn my ears that have listened to thee for so long."

This society used "you" as a respectful and more formal way of referring to someone and "thee" and "thou" as a less respectful and more informal way of referring to someone. Imogen no longer respected Iachimo. "Thee" and "thou" were used to talk to a servant or a child or a pet dog. "Thee" and "thou" could also be used when talking to a person with whom one had an intimate relationship, such as one's husband or wife. In the King James Bible, God is "Thou" because human beings can have a personal relationship with God. Imogen, however, makes it clear that she is using "thee" and "thou" to refer to Iachimo because she does not respect him. Iachimo is a newcomer to the palace and so ought to be called by the formal "you."

Imogen continued, "If thou were honorable, thou would have told this tale for a virtuous reason, not for such a contemptible end as the one thou seeks — as dishonorable as it is strange. Thou wrong a gentleman, who is as far from thy report as thou are from honor, and thou are soliciting here a lady who disdains thee as much as she does the devil."

She called again, "Pisanio!"

She then said to Iachimo, "I shall tell the King my father about thy assault. If my father thinks it fitting that an impudent, insolent foreigner should do business in his court as if he were in a Roman stew — a Roman whorehouse — and to expound his beastly mind to us, he has a court he cares little for and a daughter whom he does not respect at all."

She called again, "Pisanio!"

Iachimo had failed to seduce Imogen. Now he needed to stay out of trouble — and to not die. Kings had the power to impose capital punishment.

"Oh, happy Leonatus!" Iachimo said. "I may say the respect that your lady has for you deserves your trust, and your most perfect goodness deserves her assured faith in you."

He said to Imogen, "May you be blessed and live long! You are the wife to the worthiest gentleman that a country has ever called its own! You, his wife, are suitable only for the very worthiest! Give me your pardon. Forgive me. I have spoken these things only to learn if your marriage vows were deeply rooted, and I have discovered that they are. Those vows shall make your husband that which he is, but renewed — your lover. He is the truest mannered man. He is such a holy warlock — he uses white magic — that he enchants societies of friends. Half of the heart of every man is given to him."

Imogen forgave Iachimo and began to use "you" when speaking to him: "You make amends for what you said."

"Your husband sits among men as if he were a god who had descended from Heaven. He has a kind of honor that sets him off; his appearance is that of more than a mortal man. Do not be angry, most mighty Princess, that I have ventured to test how you would take a false report about your husband. This test has honored you by confirming your great judgment in choosing to marry so rare a gentleman — you know that your judgment in this matter cannot be wrong. The love I bear your husband drove me to fan and winnow — to test — you like this, but the gods made you, unlike all others, without chaff and unsullied. Please, I beg your pardon."

"All is well, sir," Imogen said. "You may use my power in the court as if it were yours."

"I give you my humble thanks," Iachimo said. "I had almost forgotten to ask your grace to fulfill a small request, and yet it is important, too, because it concerns your husband. He, myself, and other noble friends are partners in this particular matter."

"Please, tell me what it is."

"Some dozen of us Romans and your husband — who is the best feather of our wing — have mingled sums of money in order to buy a present for the Emperor. I, as agent for the rest, purchased the gift in France. It is a dish made of precious metal, remarkably well designed and inlaid with jewels of rich and exquisite form. The value of the dish is great, and I am somewhat anxious, being a foreigner, to have this gift placed in a safe place for now. May it please you to keep this gift to the Emperor safe for me?"

"I will do it willingly," Imogen said. "I will pawn my honor for the safekeeping of this gift. Because my husband has an interest in it, I will keep it in my bedchamber."

"It is in a trunk being looked after by my servants," Iachimo said. "I will make bold to send the trunk to you for this night only. I must go onboard ship tomorrow."

A good hostess, Imogen said, "No, no."

"Yes," Iachimo said. "I must, please. I shall fall short on what I promised if I lengthen the time of my return to Rome. From France I crossed the seas because I promised to see your grace."

"I thank you for your pains," Imogen said, "but do not sail away tomorrow!"

"Oh, I must, madam; therefore, I shall ask you, if you want to write to your husband, please do it tonight. I have taken up too much time; I must leave quickly because time is relevant to the giving of our present to the Emperor."

"I will write my husband," Imogen said. "Send your trunk to me; it shall safely be kept, and truly returned to you. You're very welcome."

CHAPTER 2

— 2.1 —

Cloten and two lords spoke together in front of King Cymbeline's palace.

"Has any man ever had such bad luck!" Cloten complained. "I threw my ball so well that it kissed — touched — the target, but then it was hit away! I had bet a hundred pounds on the game, and I cursed, and then a bastardly upstart reprimanded me for swearing, as if I had borrowed my swearwords from him and could not spend them as I pleased."

"He got nothing by criticizing you," the first lord said. "You broke his head with your ball."

The second lord thought, *If the man with the broken head had weak and watery brains like Cloten, his brains would have all run out.*

Cloten said, "When a gentleman is disposed to swear, it is not for any bystanders to curtail his oaths, is it?"

"No, my lord," the second lord said.

He thought, *Nor to crop the ears of the gentleman.*

A curtail dog is a dog with a docked or cropped — that is, cut short — tail. The second lord was thinking of cropping the ears of an ass. Cloten was an ass, but his mother was Queen, and so no one could justly criticize him and thereby improve him — no one could crop Cloten's ears.

"The dog! That son of a whore!" Cloten said. "I gave him what he deserved. I wish that he had been one of my rank!"

Cloten would have liked to fight the man in a duel instead of merely hitting him with a ball. But Cloten, a snob, believed that he could not fight the man in a duel because the man's social status was lower than his own. Of course, because Cloten's mother was the Queen, it would be very dangerous for a man of a lower social rank to duel Cloten. Anyone who killed Cloten would almost certainly be condemned to die.

The second lord thought, *Cloten said, "I wish that he had been one of my rank!" If he had been rank like Cloten, he would have stunk like a fool.*

Cloten said, "I am not vexed more at anything on the Earth — a pox on it! I had rather not be as noble as I am; they dare not fight with me because of the

Queen my mother. Every Jack-slave has his bellyful of fighting, and I must go up and down like a cock — a rooster — that nobody can match."

The second lord said quietly to himself about Cloten, "You are cock and capon, too; and you crow, cock, with your comb on."

The second lord was calling Cloten a capon — a castrated rooster that had been fattened for eating — and a fool. Fools wore coxcombs — jesters' hats — on their heads.

"What did you say?" Cloten asked.

"It is not fitting that your lordship should take on and fight every fellow that you give offence to," the second lord said.

"I know that," Cloten said, "but it is fitting that I should give offence to my inferiors. It is suitable for me to deliberately offend my inferiors."

"Yes, it is fitting for your lordship only," the second lord said.

Such an action as deliberately insulting others because they are "inferior" is fitting and suitable only for clods such as Cloten.

"Yes, that is what I am saying," Cloten replied.

The first lord asked Cloten, "Did you hear about a stranger who came to the court last night?"

"A stranger came here! I did not know that! I was not informed about it!" Cloten said.

The second lord thought, *Cloten is a strange fellow himself, and he does not know it.*

"An Italian man has come here," the first lord said, "and it is thought that he is one of Posthumus Leonatus' friends."

"Leonatus!" Cloten said, "He's a banished rascal; and this Italian's another rascal, whoever he is. Who told you about this stranger?"

"One of your lordship's pages," the first lord said.

"Is it fitting that I go to see him?" Cloten asked. "Is there any derogation in it? Will I be lowering myself?"

"You cannot derogate, my lord —" the second lord said.

He thought, — *because you cannot go any lower.*

Cloten said, "I cannot easily derogate, I think."

The second lord thought, *Everyone already knows that you are a fool; therefore, your actions, being foolish, do not derogate you. Your performing foolish actions does not lower you because people expect you to act foolishly.*

Cloten said, "Come, I'll go see this Italian. What I have lost today gambling at the game of bowls I'll win tonight from him. Come, let's go."

"I'll wait upon your lordship," the second lord said.

Cloten and the first lord exited, and the second lord stayed behind and said to himself, "I can't believe that such a crafty devil as his mother the Queen should yield the world this ass! His mother is a woman who overwhelms everyone with her brain, and this Cloten, her son, cannot subtract two from twenty, for his life, and come up with the answer eighteen. Alas, poor Princess, you divine Imogen, what you endure! You have a father who is ruled by your stepmother, who each hour forms plots. You also have a wooer — Cloten — who is more hateful than the foul exile of your dear husband and who is more hateful than that horrid act of divorce between you and your husband that he — Cloten — would make! May the Heavens hold firm the walls of your dear honor, and keep unshook that temple, your fair mind, so that you may endure and withstand such trials and may eventually enjoy your banished lord and this great land!"

Imogen was in bed, reading, just before bedtime. Iachimo's chest was in her bedchamber.

Imogen called, "Who's there? My servant Helen?"

In mythology, Helen was the name of the wife of Menelaus, King of Sparta, and she became the cause of the Trojan War after either Paris, a Prince of Troy, kidnapped her or she ran away willingly with him. Troy fell when the Greeks created the Trojan Horse, which was hollow and filled with armed Greek soldiers. The Trojans moved the Horse inside the city, and at night the Greek soldiers came out of the Horse and opened the city gates to let in the Greek army.

"I am here, if you please, madam," Helen said.

"What time is it?"

"Almost midnight, madam."

"I have read three hours then," Imogen said. "My eyes are tired. Fold down the leaf where I have stopped reading. I am going to sleep. Do not take away the candle, leave it burning, and if you can awaken by four o'clock, please wake me up. Sleep has entirely overcome me."

Helen exited.

Imogen prayed, "To your protection I commit myself, gods. Please guard me from malevolent fairies and the tempters of the night."

She fell asleep, and Iachimo came out of the trunk — the Trojan Horse — where he had hidden himself.

He said quietly to himself, "The crickets sing, and man's overworked senses repair themselves through rest. I am like our Roman Tarquin, who like me now did softly step on the rushes on the floor before he awakened the chastity he wounded."

The ancient Roman Sextus Tarquinius had raped Lucretia, an evil act that led to the overthrow of the Roman King and the establishment of a republic. Iachimo did not dare to rape Imogen — such an act would lead to bad consequences for him — but he still wanted to win the bet that he had made with her husband.

Iachimo continued, "Imogen, you are Cytherea — Venus, who was born on the island of Cythera. How splendidly you become your bed, you fresh lily, symbol of purity, for you are whiter than the sheets! I wish that I might touch you! I want only a kiss — just one kiss! Rubies unparagoned, how dearly they do it! Your lips are like rubies, and they kiss each other. It is her breathing that perfumes the chamber. The flame of the candle bows toward her because smoke follows the most beautiful. The candle flame wants to peep under her eyelids, to see the lights — the eyes — they enclose, which are now canopied under these window shutters, which are white and azure laced with blue of Heaven's own color. Her eyelids are white but have tiny blue veins.

"But let me carry out my plan. I will take note of her bedchamber so that I can describe it to her husband and convince him that I have slept with his wife. I will write everything down. Here are such and such pictures. There is the window. Such is the decoration of her bed. Here is the wall hanging. Here is a carving of figures on the mantle over the fireplace. Why, I see such and such, and the figures act out the contents of a story.

"Ah, but some personal notes about her body would be better evidence than over ten thousand notes about the items in her bedchamber; those personal notes would significantly enrich the inventory that I am writing down."

He drew the covering away from Imogen's body and said, "Oh, sleep, you mimic of death, lie heavy upon her! Let her consciousness be like that of an effigy on top of a coffin lying in a chapel! Don't wake up!"

He began to take off her bracelet, saying, "Come off! Come off!"

It easily slipped off her arm, and he said, "It is as slippery and easy to remove as the Gordian knot was hard to untie!"

The Gordian knot was incredibly intricate, and according to prophecy, whoever was able to untie it would conquer Asia. Alexander the Great "untied" the knot by cutting it with his sword.

Holding the bracelet, Iachimo said, "It is in my possession; and this will be physical evidence that will aid me as I drive her husband to distraction."

He looked at Imogen's body and said, "On her left breast is a mole with five spots like the crimson drops in the bottom of a cowslip flower. Here's a piece of evidence that is stronger than law could ever make. This secret knowledge of her body will force her husband to think that I have picked the lock and taken the treasure of her honor. I need no more evidence. It would not help make my case stronger. Why should I write this piece of evidence down? It is riveted — screwed — to my memory! She has been reading recently the tale of Tereus; here the leaf's turned down where Philomel gave up."

Imogen had been reading about Philomel, who was raped by Tereus, her brother-in-law. After raping her, he cut out her tongue to prevent her from telling anyone about the rape. However, she created a tapestry that told the story of the rape.

Iachimo was wrong when he said that Philomel had given up. Iachimo was the type of man who believes that it was a rare — perhaps nonexistent, given enough time for the seduction to take place — woman who could not be seduced. Philomel had not given up her chastity; Tereus had forcibly raped her.

Iachimo said, "I have enough evidence. I will go inside the trunk again, and shut its spring — its locking mechanism. Be swift, swift, you dragons of the night, so that dawning may bare the raven's eye!"

According to a myth, dragons drew the chariot of the Moon. Ravens are birds of omen — they are ominous — and they wake up with the dawn.

Iachimo continued, "I lodge in this trunk in fear. Although Imogen is a Heavenly angel, Hell is here."

A clock began to strike.

Iachimo counted, "One, two, three. It is time, time for me to go into the trunk!"

He went into the trunk and shut the lid.

<h1 style="text-align:center">— 2.3 —</h1>

In an antechamber adjoining Imogen's apartments, Cloten and some lords were talking.

The first lord said to Cloten, "Your lordship is the most patient man when enduring loss. You are the very coldest man who ever turned up the lowest number on a die — an ace."

"It would make any man cold to lose," Cloten said.

The first lord had used "cold" as meaning "impassive," but Cloten used the word as meaning "gloomy."

"But not every man is patient after your lordship's noble temper. You are most hot and excitable when you win," the first lord said.

"Winning will put any man into courage," Cloten said. "If I could get this foolish Imogen, I should have gold enough."

Imogen was the presumed heir to the throne, so if Cloten married her, he would almost certainly become very, very rich.

Cloten asked, "It's almost morning, isn't it?"

"It is day, my lord," the first lord replied.

"I wish the musicians I hired would come," Cloten said. "I have been advised to provide music for Imogen in the mornings. They say the music will penetrate."

The musicians arrived, and Cloten continued his indelicate puns: "Come on; tune your instruments. If you can penetrate her with your fingering, good; we'll try to penetrate her with tongue — vocal music — too. If none will do for her, then let her alone; but I'll never give up.

"First, we will hear a very excellent cleverly devised thing; afterward, a wonderfully sweet air, with admirably rich words to it, and then let her consider me as a mate."

A musician sang this song:

"Hark! Hark! The lark at Heaven's gate sings,

"And Phoebus Apollo the Sun-god begins to arise,

"His steeds to water at those springs

"Where flowers with cup-like blossoms lie.

"And closed marigold blossoms begin

When the musicians had finished playing and singing the song, Cloten said, "So, leave now. If this penetrates, I will regard your music as being better than I have regarded it. If it does not penetrate, then it is a vice in her ears, which neither horsehairs and calves' guts, nor the voice of an unpaved eunuch in addition, can ever amend."

Horsehairs were used in bowstrings, and calves' guts — intestines — were used in the strings of lutes and viols. An unpaved eunuch had no stones, aka testicles. A different kind of stones was used in paving roads.

The musicians exited.

The second lord said, "Here comes the King."

Cloten said, "I am glad I was up so late because that's the reason I was up so early — I have not gone to bed. The King — Imogen's father — cannot choose but take fatherly this service I have done."

King Cymbeline and the Queen came over to Cloten and the two lords.

Cymbeline said, "Are you waiting here at the door of our stern daughter? Won't she come out?"

Cloten said, "I have assailed her with music, but she gives no notice of it."

Cymbeline said, "The exile of her minion — Posthumus — is too new and recent. She has not yet forgotten him. Some more time must pass before she forgets him, and then she's yours."

"You owe the King, who lets go by no suitable opportunity to recommend you to his daughter," the Queen said. "Prepare yourself to pursue her in a methodical fashion. Take advantage of favorable opportunities. Whenever she rejects you, pursue her more doggedly. Seem as if you were inspired by love to do those duties that you offer to her. Obey her in everything except when she rejects you and commands you to let her alone — that command you shall ignore and be senseless to."

By "senseless," the Queen meant "incapable of hearing."

"Senseless!" Cloten said, misunderstanding her. "I am not senseless! I am not a fool!"

A messenger entered the room.

The messenger said to King Cymbeline, "Sir, ambassadors from Rome have come. The main ambassador is the Roman general Caius Lucius."

Using the royal plural, Cymbeline replied, "He is a worthy fellow, although he comes here now with an angry purpose, but that's no fault of his. We must receive him in accordance with the honor of his sender, and we must treat him well because of his past goodness to us."

He said to Cloten, "Our dear stepson, when you have said good morning to Imogen, attend the Queen and us; we shall have need to employ you in escorting this Roman."

He then said, "Let us go, our Queen."

Everyone except Cloten exited.

Cloten said to himself, "If Imogen is up, I'll speak with her; if she is not up, then let her lie still and dream."

He knocked on her door and said loudly, "Open, please!"

Then he said quietly to himself, "I know her female servants are around her. What if I line one of their hands with money as a bribe? It is gold that buys admittance, often it does; yes, and gold makes the virgin goddess Diana's gamekeepers be false to their vows and yield their deer to the stand of the stealer."

The Roman goddess Diana was a hunter who fiercely guarded her virginity. A mortal hunter named Actaeon once accidentally saw her bathing naked; Diana turned his body into that of a stag although he kept his human mind, and his own hounds tore him to pieces. Cloten believed that gold would make the female servants of Imogen, who carefully guarded her chastity, deliver her into his hands. As he often did, he made an indecent pun. A hunter's stand was a spot from which the hunter could shoot game; a stand was also an erection.

Cloten continued, "And it is gold that kills the honest man and saves the thief; no, sometimes gold hangs both thief and honest man. What can't gold do and undo? I will make one of her female servants be a lawyer — an advocate — for me, for I do not yet understand the case myself."

The word "case" meant "lawsuit," and it was slang for "vagina." The indecent meaning of what Cloten had said was that his erection was not yet under Imogen's vagina; it was not yet under standing — that is, standing under — it.

He knocked again on Imogen's door and said, "Open, please!"

As one of Imogen's female servants opened the door, she asked, "Who's knocking?"

Cloten replied, "A gentleman."

"No more than that?" the female servant replied, coming out of Imogen's bedchamber.

"Yes, more than that. I am a gentlewoman's son," replied Cloten, who was expensively dressed.

"That's more than some men, whose tailors are as expensive as yours, can justly boast of. What's your lordship's pleasure?"

"Your lady's person is my pleasure. Is she ready?"

Cloten was asking if Imogen was up and decently dressed, but the female servant misunderstood, perhaps deliberately, the meaning of "ready," as she answered, "Yes, she is ready to stay in her bedchamber."

Cloten held out some money to her and said, "There is gold for you; sell me your good report."

"What!" the female servant said. "Sell you my own good report? Sell you what people say about me? Sell you my good reputation? Or do you want me to report — to say — good things about you to Imogen?"

Imogen walked through the door, and the female servant said, "The Princess!"

Cloten said to Imogen, "Good morning, fairest lady. Stepsister, give me your sweet hand."

The female servant exited.

"Good morning, sir," Imogen replied. "You take too many pains for purchasing nothing but trouble; the thanks I give you are to tell you that I am poor of thanks and scarcely can spare them."

"Still, I swear I love you," Cloten said.

"If you had just said you love me instead of swearing you love me, it would be the same to me. If you continue to swear, your recompense will continue to be the same — I will ignore what you say."

"This is no answer," Cloten said.

"I would say nothing to you except that I am afraid that if I am silent, you may say that I have yielded to your love. Please, spare me from speaking to you. Truly, I am afraid that I will give you discourtesy that will equal your best kindness. One of your 'great knowledge' should learn, being taught, forbearance."

Imogen was being sarcastic when she said that Cloten possessed "great knowledge."

"If I were to leave you in your madness, it would be my sin," said Cloten, who believed that it would be mad for Imogen to reject him. "Therefore, I will not leave you."

"Fools are not mad folks," Imogen said.

She meant that she might be a fool for talking to Cloten, but she was not mad, and therefore Cloten could leave her.

Misunderstanding as usual, Cloten asked, "Are you calling me a fool?"

"As I am 'mad,' I do," Imogen said. "You call me mad; I call you a fool. If you'll exercise self-restraint and leave me alone, I'll no longer be mad; that will cure us both. I am very sorry, sir, that you make me forget a lady's manners. A lady ought to be mostly silent, but I have been very verbal. So that I need not speak further words to you, learn now, once and for all, that I, who know my own heart, do here say, very truthfully, that I do not care for you, and I am so close to lacking Christian charity that I must — am forced to — accuse myself of hating you. I wish that you could understand what I feel without my expressing it verbally."

"You sin against obedience, which you owe your father," Cloten said. "You made a marriage contract without the approval of your father, and so it is only a pretend marriage contract that you made with Posthumus, that base wretch, who was brought up with alms and fostered with cold dishes, with leftover scraps of food from the court — it is no marriage contract, not at all. Such a marriage contract is allowed for lowly people — yet who is more lowly than Posthumus? — to knit their souls in a marriage arranged by themselves only. Relying on these people are no dependents other than brats and beggars.

"You, however, are not permitted that freedom because of your importance. You will inherit the crown, and you must not dishonor and soil its precious reputation by either marrying a base slave, a good-for-nothing, worthless man fit only for the uniform of a servant, for wearing the cloth of a squire, for being the servant who keeps the pantry, or by marrying a man who is not as eminent as these men are."

Imogen replied, "Profane fellow, if you were the son of Jupiter and no more but what you are besides that, you would be too base to be Posthumus' servant. If social rank were based on merit and not on birth, Posthumus would be a King and you would be an assistant executioner in his Kingdom. As a hangman's apprentice, you would be raised high enough in status that other people would envy and hate you for being promoted so well. People would envy and hate you because they would think that you had been promoted beyond what you deserve."

"I hope the south wind rots Posthumus!" Cloten said.

In this culture, the south wind was thought to be damp and unhealthy.

Using the less respectful "thou" to refer to Cloten, Imogen said, "He can never meet more misfortune than for thou to say his name. His meanest garment — his underwear — that has ever hugged his body is dearer to me than all the hairs above you if they were to be made such men as you."

Suddenly noticing that the bracelet that Posthumus had given to her was missing from her arm, Imogen said, "What!"

She called, "Pisanio!"

Pisanio came to her.

Cloten muttered, "'His garment!' What the devil —"

Imogen said to Pisanio, "Hurry immediately to my servant Dorothy—"

Cloten muttered, "'His garment!'"

Imogen said, "I am haunted by a fool. Something has happened that frightens — and worse, angers — me. Go tell Dorothy to search for a bracelet that accidentally and too carelessly has left my arm. It was your master's gift to me. May I be cursed if I would lose it for the income of any King who is in Europe. I think I saw it this morning; I am confident that it was on my arm last night — I kissed it. I hope that it has not gone to make my husband think that I kiss anyone but he."

"We will find it," Pisanio said.

"I hope so," Imogen replied. "Go and search for it."

Pisanio exited.

Cloten said to Imogen, "You have insulted me. 'His meanest garment!'"

"Yes, I said that, sir. If you want to make a lawsuit out of it, call me as a witness to it."

"I will inform your father," Cloten said.

"Inform your mother, too," Imogen replied. Sarcastically, she said, "She's my 'good lady,'" and then added, "and will think, I think, only the worst of me. So, I leave you, sir, to the worst discontent and unhappiness."

Imogen exited.

Alone, Cloten said, "I'll be revenged on her. 'His meanest garment!' Well!"

Posthumus and Philario talked together in a room of Philario's house in Rome.

"Don't worry about it, sir," Posthumus said to Philario. "I wish I were as sure of winning over King Cymbeline as I am sure that Imogen's honor will remain intact."

"What are you doing to make King Cymbeline your friend?"

"Nothing, except watching the passage of time, quaking in his present wintery mood and wishing that warmer days would come. With these seared, withered hopes of mine, I barely repay your friendship to me; if my hopes of being reconciled to King Cymbeline fail, I must die much your debtor."

"Your true goodness and your company more than pay me for all I can do," Philario said. "By this time, your King Cymbeline has heard from great Augustus Caesar, first Emperor of Rome. Caius Lucius will thoroughly do his commission of delivering Caesar's message, and I think your King Cymbeline will grant that the tribute is owed and pay the as-yet-unpaid tribute, or else he will look upon our Roman legions, who recently caused the Britons much grief."

Posthumus replied, "I believe, although I am not a politician or likely ever to be one, that this will cause a war; and you shall sooner hear that the legions now in France have landed in our courageous Britain than you will have news of even a penny of tribute paid. Our countrymen are more organized than when Julius Caesar smiled at their lack of skill, but found their courage worthy of his frowning at. The Britons' discipline, now mingled with their courage, will make known to those who test them that they are people whose existence improves the world."

Philario looked up and said, "Look! Iachimo is here!"

Posthumus said to him, "The swiftest deer have carried you quickly by land; and the winds of all the corners of the world have kissed your sails and made your ship nimble."

"Welcome, sir," Philario said.

Posthumus said to Iachimo, "I hope the shortness of the answer you got from my wife when you attempted to seduce her made the speediness of your return necessary."

Iachimo replied, "Your lady is one of the most beautiful whom I have looked upon."

"And also the best and most virtuous, or let her beauty look through a window to allure false hearts and be false with them," Posthumus said.

In this culture, prostitutes displayed themselves in windows to allure customers.

"Here is a letter for you from your wife," Iachimo said, handing Posthumus a letter.

"The subject matter of the letter is good, I trust," Posthumus said.

"It is very likely," Iachimo replied.

He had not read the letter, which was sealed. He was hoping that Imogen had not written her husband that Iachimo had tried to seduce her, but had failed.

Posthumus scanned the letter as Philario asked Iachimo, "Was Caius Lucius in the British court when you were there?"

"He was expected, but he had not yet arrived."

Having scanned the letter, Posthumus said, "All is still well."

He then held out the hand wearing the diamond ring he had bet and asked Iachimo, "Does this diamond sparkle as it used to? Or is it too dull for you to wear?"

"If I had lost our bet, I would have lost the worth of the ring in gold because I bet my gold against your ring," Iachimo said. "I would make a journey twice as far, to enjoy a second night of such sweet shortness that was mine in Britain, for I have won the ring."

"The diamond ring is too hard to come by," Posthumus said.

"Not at all," Iachimo said, "because your wife is so easy."

"Sir," Posthumus said, "do not make a joke out of your loss. I hope you know that we must not continue to be friends."

"Good sir, we must continue to be friends, if you keep the terms of the bet we made. Had I not brought the carnal knowledge of your wife home with me, I grant that we would have to fight a duel, but I now say that I am the winner of your wife's honor, and so I have also won the ring. However, I say that I have not wronged either her or you because I have done nothing that you two did not give me permission to do."

Posthumus had given Iachimo permission to attempt to seduce his wife, and Iachimo had made the attempt. Posthumus' wife, Imogen, had not given Iachimo to sleep with her, and he had not slept with her.

Posthumus said, "If you can prove that you have tasted my wife in bed, my hand of friendship and my ring are yours; if not, the foul opinion you had of my wife's pure honor gains or loses either your sword or mine, or masterless leaves both swords to whoever shall find them. Either I shall kill you or you shall kill me or we shall kill each other."

"Sir, my evidence, being so near the truth as I will make it, must first induce you to believe," Iachimo said. "I will confirm the strength of my evidence with an oath, but I don't doubt that you will give me permission not to swear an oath that my evidence is true because you will find that my evidence is so strong that you don't need an oath to believe it."

Iachimo's "evidence" was strong enough to convince Posthumus that Imogen had been unfaithful to him, but Iachimo's "evidence" was not true.

"Proceed," Posthumus said. "Give me the evidence."

"First, her bedchamber — where, I confess, I did not sleep, but I confess that I had something that was well worth keeping awake for — had a hanging tapestry made of silk and silver thread. It told the story of when proud Cleopatra met her Roman, Mark Antony, and the Cydnus River swelled above its banks, either because of the weight of the many boats on it or from pride of being Cleopatra and Antony's meeting place. This was a piece of work so splendidly done, so rich, that I did not know which was greater — its workmanship or its value. I wondered how it could be so rarely and exactly wrought, since the true life on it was —"

Posthumus interrupted, "— this description is accurate, but you might have heard about the tapestry here, from me, or from some other person."

"More particular details about your wife's bedchamber must prove my knowledge," Iachimo said.

"So they must," Posthumus said, "or do your honor injury."

"The fireplace is on the south wall of her bedchamber, and the statues on the mantle depict the virgin goddess Diana bathing. I have never seen figures so likely to speak; the sculptor was like another Mother Nature, but silent; the sculptor outdid Mother Nature, except that his sculptures did not move or speak."

"This is another thing that you might have learned without seeing it because this artwork is much spoken about," Posthumus said.

"The ceiling of her bedchamber is elaborately adorned with golden angels. Her andirons — I had forgotten them — were two winking Cupids made of silver. Each was standing on one foot and ingeniously depicted leaning against their torches."

"You think that this is evidence that you have taken my wife's honor!" Posthumus said sarcastically. "Let it be granted you have seen all this — and I have to praise your memory — still the description of what is in my wife's bedchamber is no evidence that you have won the wager."

"Then, if you can, grow pale," Iachimo said as he took Imogen's bracelet out of a pocket and showed it to Posthumus. "I ask permission to air this bracelet. See it!"

He replaced the bracelet in his pocket and said, "And now I have put it up again. It must be married to your diamond ring. I'll keep them both together."

"By Jove!" Posthumus said, turning pale. "Let me see that again. Is that the bracelet I left with her?"

"Sir, I thank her for this bracelet," Iachimo said. "She stripped it from her arm; I see her doing it now. Her pretty action was worth more than her gift, and yet her action enriched the bracelet, too. She gave it to me, and she said that she had once valued it."

Posthumus said, "Maybe she plucked it off to send it to me."

"Did she write that in her letter to you, sir?" Iachimo said.

"Oh, no, no, no!" Posthumus said. "What you say about my wife is true. Here, take this, too."

He handed Iachimo his diamond ring and said, "It is a basilisk to my eyes. It kills me when I look at it."

A basilisk is a mythological serpent whose look can kill.

Posthumus ranted, "Let there be no honor where there is beauty; no truth, where there is only an outward appearance; and no love, where there is another man. May the vows of women be no more binding to the men they are made to than women are bound to their virtue — which is not at all! Oh, my wife is unfaithful and cheating beyond measure!"

"Be calm, sir," Philario said, "and take your ring back again. Iachimo has not yet won it. It may be probable she lost her bracelet; or who knows if one of her women, being corrupted, has stolen it from her?"

"That is very true," Posthumus said, "and in one of those two ways, I hope, he came by her bracelet. Give me back my ring. Tell me something about my wife's body that will be more evidence than this bracelet because this bracelet was stolen."

"By Jupiter, I swear that I got it from her arm," Iachimo said.

"Listen!" Posthumus said to Philario. "He swears; he swears by Jupiter! What he says must be true since he swears by the supreme god!"

He gave the diamond ring back to Iachimo, saying, "Keep the ring — what you say is true."

He then said, "I am sure that my wife would not lose her bracelet. Her attendants are all sworn to obey her and be honorable. Could they be induced to steal it! Induced by a stranger! No, Iachimo has enjoyed my wife in bed. The symbol of her cheating is this ring. She has bought the name of whore grievously at great cost."

He said to Iachimo, "There, take your winnings; and may all the fiends of Hell divide themselves between you and my wife, Imogen!"

"Sir, be calm," Philario said to Posthumus. "This evidence is not strong enough to be believed about one you have thought so well about —"

Posthumus interrupted, "— never talk about not believing it. Imogen has been colted — mounted — by him."

"If you seek further evidence," Iachimo said, "under her breast — which is worth squeezing — lies a mole, which is very proud of that most delicate place of residence. By my life, I kissed it; and it immediately made me hungry to feed again, though I was already full. You remember this mole — this stain and imperfection — on her?"

"Yes," Posthumus said, "and it confirms another stain, as big as Hell can hold, even if she had no other stain than that."

"Do you want to hear more?" Iachimo asked.

"Spare your arithmetic," Posthumus said. "Don't count the turns. Once, and a million, are both enough!"

"I'll be sworn —" Iachimo began to say.

Posthumus interrupted, "— no swearing. If you will swear you have not done the deed with my wife, you lie, and I will kill you if you deny that you have made me a cuckold."

"I'll deny nothing," Iachimo said.

"Oh, I wish that I had her here so I could tear her limb from limb!" Posthumus said. "I will go there and do it ... in the court ... in front of her father! I'll do something —"

He exited.

Philario said to Iachimo, "He is quite beside himself! He has lost all self-control! You have won the bet. Let's follow him, and turn aside the present wrath he has against himself. We don't want him to hurt himself."

"With all my heart," Iachimo said.

Posthumus managed to elude Philario and Iachimo. Alone in another room of Philario's house, he said to himself, "Is there no way for men to come into existence but women must be half-workers and give birth to men? We are all bastards. That most venerable man whom I called my father was I know not where when I was created — stamped like a coin. Some coiner with his tools — one of them biological and located below his waist — made me a counterfeit. Yet my mother seemed to be the chaste goddess Diana of that time as my wife seemed to be the nonpareil of this time. Oh, I want vengeance, vengeance!

"She restrained me from enjoying my lawful pleasure of her and often begged me to be patient. She begged me with a modesty so rosy that the sweet view of her modesty might well have warmed the god Saturn, who is ancient and cold and melancholy. I thought that she was as chaste as unsunned snow. Oh, all the devils! This sallow-faced Iachimo, in an hour — was it an entire hour? Or less? Or immediately? Perhaps he did not even speak to her, but like a full-acorned boar, a German one, well fed and with huge testicles, cried 'Oh!' and mounted her and found no opposition but what he expected should oppose him and what she should from encounter guard."

Had Posthumus consummated the marriage with Imogen? Perhaps he had lied about seeing Imogen's mole. After all, Iachimo had made a mistake about the mole's location. When he had seen the mole, he had said that it was located on her breast, but he had just now told Posthumus that the mole was located under her breast. The opposition that Posthumus thought that Iachimo had expected could have been Imogen's hymen. Imogen may not have wanted to sleep with Posthumus until after she received her father's approval of the marriage.

Posthumus continued, "I wish I could find the woman's part in me! There is no provocation that leads to vice in man, but I state that it comes from the woman's part. If the vice is lying, it comes from the woman's part. The same is true of flattering, deceiving, lustful and rank thoughts, revenges, ambitions, covetings, varieties of sexual excesses, disdain, lustful longing, slanders, inconstancy — all faults that may be named, nay, all that Hell knows. Why, they are women's, in part or all — but rather, all, because even when it comes to vice women are not constant and loyal but are always exchanging one vice, which is only a minute old, for another vice that is not half as old as that.

"I'll write against women, detest them, and curse them, yet it shows greater skill in a true hate to pray that women have their will. Not even devils can plague them better."

CHAPTER 3

— 3.1 —

In a hall of King Cymbeline's palace, Cymbeline, the Queen, Cloten, and some lords were meeting with Caius Lucius, who was one of Caesar Augustus' generals and ambassadors. Many of Caius Lucius' attendants and Cymbeline's attendants were also present. Cymbeline and Caius Lucius liked each other, but it was possible that they would soon be on opposite sides in a war between Britain and Rome.

King Cymbeline said, "Now tell us, what does Augustus Caesar want with us?"

Caius Lucius replied, "When Julius Caesar, the memory of whom still lives in men's minds and who will forever be spoken about, was in this Britain and conquered it, King Cassibelan, your great-uncle — who was famous because of Caesar's praises, and whose feats entirely deserved both the praise and the fame — granted Rome a tribute both from him and from his successors, three thousand pounds annually, which by you lately has not been paid."

The Queen said, "And, to stop the astonishment that this action causes, let me say that the tribute shall be paid no longer."

Cloten said, "There will be many Caesars before there is another Caesar like Julius. Britain is a world by itself; and we will pay nothing for wearing our own noses."

He was mocking the Roman nose, which often had a prominent bridge.

The Queen said to Caius Lucius, "In Julius Caesar's day, the Romans had the opportunity to make the Britons pay tribute. Now the Britons have the opportunity to stop paying tribute."

She said to her husband, the King, "Sir, my liege, remember the Kings your ancestors, together with the natural threatening appearance of your isle, which stands like the park of Neptune, god of the sea, enclosed as if within ribs and fenced in with unscalable rocks and roaring waters, and with quicksands that will not bear your enemies' boats, but will suck them down all the way to the topmast. A kind of conquest Julius Caesar made here, but he did not here make his brag of 'I came' and 'I saw' and 'I conquered.' Instead, with shame

— it was the first time that shame ever touched him — he was carried from off our coast, twice beaten; and his ships — poor inexperienced toys! — upon our terrible seas moved upon their waves like eggshells and cracked as easily as eggshells against our rocks. This brought much joy to the famed Cassibelan, who was once at the point — oh, Lady Fortune, you harlot! — of mastering Julius Caesar's sword. To celebrate, Cassibelan made Lud's town bright with rejoicing fires, and Britons strutted with courage."

Lud's town would in a later age be known as London.

Cloten said, "Come, we will pay no more tribute. Our Kingdom is stronger than it was at that time; and, as I said, there are no more such Caesars as Julius Caesar. Other Caesars may have crooked noses, but none own such straight, strong arms as did Julius."

"Stepson, let your mother finish speaking," Cymbeline said to Cloten.

Cloten continued, "We have yet many among us who can grip a sword as hard as Cassibelan. I do not say I am one of them, but I have a hand. Why tribute? Why should we pay tribute? If Caesar Augustus can hide the Sun from us with a blanket, or put the Moon in his pocket, we will pay him tribute in return for light; otherwise, sir, we will pay no more tribute, if you please."

King Cymbeline said, "You must know, Caius Lucius, that until the injurious and insulting Romans extorted this tribute from us, we were free. Caesar's ambition, which swelled so much that it almost stretched the sides of the world, against all reason here put the yoke upon us; to shake off that yoke is fitting for a warlike people, whom we reckon ourselves to be."

Cloten and the other lords present said, "We do."

Cymbeline said to Caius Lucius, "Say, then, to Caesar Augustus, that our ancestor was that Mulmutius who established our laws, whose use the sword of Caesar has too much mangled, and whose restoration and free exercise shall, by the power we hold, be our good deed, although Rome thereby be made angry. Mulmutius made our laws, and he was the first man of Britain who put his brows within a golden crown and called himself King."

Caius Lucius replied, "I am sorry, Cymbeline, that I am to pronounce Augustus Caesar — who has more Kings acting as his servants than you yourself have domestic servants — your enemy. Receive this sentence from me, then. In Caesar's name I pronounce war and destruction against you. Expect

Roman fury that cannot be resisted. Having thus delivered this sentence from Caesar Augustus, I now personally thank you for what you have done for me."

"You are welcome, Caius," Cymbeline said. "Your Caesar knighted me. I spent much of my youth serving under him. From him I gathered honor. Since he seeks to take that honor from me, I will resist him, of necessity, to the utmost. I am perfectly aware that the Pannonians in Hungary and the Dalmatians on the Adriatic Sea are now up in arms and fighting for their liberties; this is a precedent that would show the Britons to be cold and apathetic if they did not follow it. Caesar Augustus shall not find us cold and apathetic."

Caius Lucius said, "Let the outcome of the war do the speaking."

"His majesty bids you welcome," Cloten said. "Stay with us and enjoy yourself a day or two, or longer. If you seek us afterwards on other terms, you shall find us within the salt water that girdles our island. If you beat us out of our island, it is yours; if you fall in the venture, our crows shall fare the better because of feasting on you; and that's all that needs to be said."

"So be it, sir," Caius Lucius replied.

King Cymbeline said, "I know your master's message, and through you he will know mine. Our official business is over. All that remains to be done now is for me to say to you, personally, 'Welcome!'"

Pisanio, who had two letters from Posthumus Leonatus, was reading the one addressed to him.

He said to himself, "What! Imogen accused of adultery? Why didn't you write about what monster is her accuser? Leonatus! Oh, master! What a strange infection has fallen into your ear! What treacherous Italian, as poisonous-tongued as poisonous-handed, has prevailed on your too ready hearing?"

Italians had a reputation for being talented in the use of poisons.

Pisanio continued, "Imogen disloyal! No! She's being punished for being honest and loyal and true, and she endures, more like a goddess than a wife, such assaults as would conquer some who are virtuous. Oh, my master! Your mind compared to her mind is now as low as were your fortunes. What! You write that I should murder her! I should do that because of my respect for you and my loyalty to you and my vows to serve you! I? Kill her? I? Spill her blood? If this is what it takes to do good service, then never let me be thought to do good service. How do I look? How can I seem to lack so much humanity that it appears that I would commit the murder that Posthumus Leonatus tells me to commit?"

He read part of the letter out loud, "*Do it. The letter that I have sent to her shall convince her to do something that will give you the opportunity to kill her.*"

He said, "Oh, damned paper! You are black as the ink that's on you! Letter, you are a worthless trifle that lacks human feeling and empathy! Letter, are you a confederate for this act of murder, and yet you look so virgin-like on the outside?"

He looked up and said, "Here Imogen comes. I will pretend to be ignorant of what I am commanded to do."

Imogen walked over and said, "Hello, Pisanio!"

"Madam, here is a letter from my lord."

"From whom? Your lord? He is my lord and husband: Posthumus Leonatus! Oh, learned indeed would be an astrologer who knew the stars as well as I do my husband's handwriting. Such an astrologer would reveal the future. You good gods, let what is contained in this letter taste of love, of my lord's health, of his happiness except for our being apart — let that grieve him. Some griefs are curative; that is one of them because it ministers to love. Let him be happy in everything except our being apart!"

Starting to break the beeswax that sealed — locked the contents of — the letter, she said, "Good wax, by your leave. Blest be you bees that make these locks of counsel! Lovers and men who have made dangerous contracts do not regard letters similarly. A letter can result in a defaulter's being cast in prison, yet a letter can allow a lover to hold the writing of young Cupid. Please let this letter bear good news, gods!"

She read Posthumus' letter out loud, "*Justice, and the wrath of your father, if he should capture me in his Kingdom, could not be so cruel to me, as you, dearest of creatures, would completely renew and restore me with your eyes.*"

Posthumus was writing a deceptive letter, but he could not prevent his anger from showing up in it. The beginning of the letter read, "*Justice, and the wrath of your father, if he should capture me in his Kingdom, could not be so cruel to me, as you ....*" But then he continued the letter and wrote that Imogen would be able to completely renew and restore him by looking at him.

Imogen continued to read the letter out loud, "*Take notice that I am in Wales, at the harbor town Milford Haven. What your own love will advise you to do after reading this, do. So he wishes you all happiness, you who remain loyal to his vow, and he wishes your increasing in love. LEONATUS POSTHUMUS.*"

Imogen, who immediately knew that she wanted to go to Wales, and who was so happy that she spoke excitedly and jumbled her thoughts, said, "Oh, for a horse with wings! Do you hear, Pisanio? Posthumus is at Milford Haven. Read this letter, and tell me how far it is to Milford Haven. If a person on ordinary business may plod it in a week, why can't I glide there in a day? Then, true Pisanio ... who longs, like me, to see your lord; who longs ... let me amend that ... who does not long like me ... yet who longs, but in a less longing way ... oh, not like me because my longing is beyond beyond ... tell me, and speak quickly because the adviser of a lover should fill the holes of hearing ... the ears ... to the smothering of the sense ... how far it is to this same blessed Milford Haven, and as we travel tell me how Wales was made so happy as to inherit such a haven, but first of all tell me how we may steal away from here, and how we shall excuse the gap that we shall make in time, from our going away until our return, but first, tell me how we shall get away from here. But why should we find an excuse for something we have not yet done? We'll talk about that excuse later. Please, tell me how many scores of miles can we ride between one hour and the next?"

Pisanio replied, "One score between sunrise and sunset, madam, is enough for you."

Knowing that Posthumus would not be at Milford Haven when they arrived, he thought, *And too much, too.*

Imogen said, "Why, one who rode to his execution, man, could never go so slowly. I have heard of people betting on horse races, where horses have been nimbler than the sands that run through an hourglass. But this delay is foolery. Go tell my woman servant to feign a sickness. Say that she'll go home to her father, and immediately provide for me traveling clothes, no costlier than would be suitable for the housewife of a franklin."

A franklin is a landowner below the rank of gentry.

"Madam, you had better consider carefully what you are doing," Pisanio said.

"I see the road that is in front of me, man," Imogen said. "I don't see what is on the right or what is on the left. The right and the left and what is in the future have a fog around them that I cannot look through. Go now, please, and do what I told you to do. The only accessible path is the one that leads to Milford Haven."

Belarius, Guiderius, and Arviragus came out of the cave that was their home in the mountainous country of Wales. A lord who had been banished from Cymbeline's court, Belarius was using the name of Morgan. Guiderius and Arviragus were actually the kidnapped biological sons of Cymbeline, although they thought that they were the biological sons of Morgan; their names as Morgan's sons were Polydore and Cadwal. Guiderius (Polydore) was the older of the two.

Belarius (Morgan) said as he came out of the cave, "This is an excellent day not to stay at home, especially a home with a roof as low as ours! Stoop, boys; this entrance instructs you how to adore the Heavens and bows you to a morning's holy worship. In contrast to our entranceway, the gates of monarchs are arched so high that Muslim giants may strut through and keep their impious turbans on, without bowing a good morning to the Sun. Hail, you fair Heaven! We live in a cave in the rock, yet we do not treat you as harshly as those who live better than we do."

Guiderius (Polydore) said, "Hail, Heaven!"

Arviragus (Cadwal) said, "Hail, Heaven!"

"Now for our mountain sport," Belarius (Morgan) said. "Climb up yonder hill; your legs are young. I'll tread this flat land. Consider, when you from above perceive me to look like the size of a crow, that it is one's position, including social as well as physical, that lessens and enhances a person, and you may then revolve in your mind what tales I have told you about courts, about Princes, about tricks in war. Any act of service in public life is not service simply because it is done, but it becomes service as a result of being acknowledged. What matters is not what you have done, but what your superiors think you have done.

"When we think about things in this way, we can profit from everything we see, and often, to our comfort, we shall find that the dung beetle is in a safer fortress than is the full-winged eagle."

In part, this meant that the dung beetle was safer because it lived in a humble abode and stayed away from the lavish abode of the court; however, Belarius (Morgan) was familiar with Aesop's fable of the dung beetle and the eagle: Once an eagle was chasing a hare, who appealed to a dung beetle — the only creature around — for help. The dung beetle promised to help the hare, but the eagle ignored the dung beetle's appeals for mercy and killed and devoured the hare in front of the dung beetle. Thereafter, the dung beetle sought to avenge the hare. The eagle would lay its eggs in a nest, and the dung beetle would go to the nest and push the eagle's eggs out of the nest to the ground, where they broke. The eagle appealed to Jupiter, King of gods and men, for help. Jupiter held the eagle's eggs in his lap, thinking they would be safe there. But the dung beetle took flight, carrying a ball of dung, which it dropped in Jupiter's lap. Without thinking, Jupiter stood up to get the ball of dung off him, and the eagle's eggs fell to the ground and broke. Moral: Despise no one. No one is so small that he or she cannot avenge an insult.

Belarius (Morgan) continued, "Oh, this life is nobler than a life of providing service only to be rebuked, this life is richer than a life of accepting bribes and then doing nothing, and this life is prouder than a life of wearing unpaid-for silk that rustles. People who wear unpaid-for silk will be saluted by their tailors, who make them fine, but yet the finely dressed people never succeed in paying off their bills. That is no life compared to our life."

"You speak from your experience of life," Guiderius (Polydore) said. "We — Cadwal and me — are poor and unfledged. We have never winged away from the view of the nest, nor do we know what the air is like away from home. Perhaps this life is best, if quiet life is the best; it is sweeter to you, who have known a sharper life. It is well suited to your stiff old age, but to us it is a life of ignorance, with all traveling done while dreaming in bed. It is a prison for a debtor, who does not dare to step out of sanctuary because he will be arrested."

"What will we speak about when we are as old as you?" Arviragus (Cadwal) asked. "When we shall hear the rain and wind beat during a dark December, how, in this our confining cave, shall we discourse the freezing hours away? We have seen nothing. We are like beasts. We are as subtle as the fox when it comes to seeking prey for food. We are as warlike as the wolf when it comes to what we eat. Our valor is to chase what flees away from us. We make our cage a choir, as does the imprisoned bird, and we freely sing in our bondage."

"How you speak!" Belarius (Morgan) said. "If you only knew the city's financial practices and had suffered from them! The art of the court is as hard to leave as it is to keep up. Attempting to climb to the top results in falling, or else the climb is so slippery that the fear of falling is as bad as falling. Think about the toil of the war, a pain that only seems to seek out danger in the name of fame and honor, both of which die in the search, and has as often a slanderous epitaph as a reputation for having done the right thing — many times a person who does the right thing is given what he does not deserve as recompense. What's worse, the person who is censured must bow as he is censured!

"Boys, the world may read my story on my body. My body is marked with Roman swords, and my military reputation was once first among the best soldiers of note. King Cymbeline respected me, and when a soldier was the theme of conversation, my name was not far off. At that time I was like a tree whose boughs bent with fruit, but in one night, a storm or robbery — call it what you will — shook down my mellow hanging fruit, and also my leaves, and left me bare to the weather."

"Uncertain favor!" Guiderius (Polydore) said.

"My fault was nothing — as I have told you often — but two villains, whose false oaths prevailed before my perfect honor, swore to Cymbeline that I was allied with the Romans," Belarius (Morgan) said. "And so I was banished, and for twenty years this rock and these regions have been my world. Here I have lived in honest freedom and paid more pious debts to Heaven than in all the early years of my life.

"But go up to the mountains! I have not been speaking hunters' language. Whoever first strikes the animal we shall eat shall be the lord of the feast; to him the other two shall minister, and we will fear no poison, which is a fear of those who live in greater state than we do. I'll meet you in the valleys."

Guiderius (Polydore) and Arviragus (Cadwal) exited to begin the hunt.

Alone, Belarius (Morgan) said to himself, "How hard it is to hide the sparks of nature! These boys don't know that they are sons to the King, nor does Cymbeline dream that they are alive. They think they are my sons; and although they were raised up humbly in the cave with the ceiling that is so low that they must bow, their thoughts reach the roofs of palaces, and nature prompts them even in simple and low things to act much more nobly than others are capable of doing.

"This Polydore is the heir of Cymbeline and Britain, and the King his father called him Guiderius. By Jove, when I sit on my three-foot stool and tell stories of the warlike feats I have done, Guiderius' spirit joins and acts out my story.

When I say, 'Thus my enemy fell, and thus I set my foot on his neck,' then the Princely blood flows in his cheek, he sweats, he strains his young sinews, and he puts himself in the posture that acts out my words.

"The younger brother, Cadwal, who was named Arviragus by Cymbeline, with equally as good acting as his older brother strikes life into my speech and shows much more his own imagination."

An animal rustled nearby and Belarius (Morgan) said, "Listen, the game is roused!"

He then said, "Oh, Cymbeline! Heaven and my conscience know that you unjustly banished me, whereupon I stole your babes when they were three and two years old, thinking to deprive you of having your sons succeed you as King of Britain, just as you deprived me of my lands."

He looked upward, and addressed the boys' wet nurse (a woman who breastfed the boys when they were infants), who was now deceased, "Euriphile, you were their wet nurse; they thought that you were their biological mother, and every day they honor your grave. They think that I, myself, Belarius, who am now called Morgan, is their natural father."

He heard more rustling in the bushes and said, "The game is afoot. It's time to hunt."

Pisanio and Imogen talked together in the country near Milford Haven.

Imogen said, "You told me, when we dismounted from our horses, that the place where I would meet my husband was near at hand. When I was born, my mother never longed to see me for the first time as much as I long now to see my husband. Pisanio! Man! Where is Posthumus? What is in your mind that makes you stare at me like that? Why do you sigh so deeply? A figure in a painting who looked as you do now would be thought to be a thing perplexed beyond self-explication. Wear a less fear-inspiring face before mental wildness conquers my staider and calmer senses. What's the matter?"

Pisanio gave her Posthumus' letter to him — the one in which Posthumus had told him to murder Imogen.

Imogen asked, "Why tender you that paper to me, with a look that is so untender? If it is summer — good — news, smile. If the news is winterly, and bad, you should keep the countenance you have now."

Pisanio did not smile.

Imogen looked at the letter and said, "My husband's handwriting! That drug-damned Italy has been too crafty for him, and he's in some tough spot!"

She said to Pisanio, "Speak, man! Your tongue may take away some of the shock of reading the letter, which otherwise might kill me!"

"Please, read the letter," Pisanio said, "and you shall find that I am a wretched man, a thing that is the most disdained by Lady Fortune."

Imogen read the letter out loud: "*Pisanio, Imogen has played the strumpet in my bed; the testimonies that this is true lie bleeding in me. I speak not out of weak surmises, but from proof as strong as my grief and as certain as I expect to get my revenge. That part you, Pisanio, must act for me, if your faith is not tainted by the breach of her faith. Let your own hands take away her life. I shall give you the opportunity to kill her at Milford Haven. She has my letter, which will lead her there. If you fear to strike her dead at Milford Haven and to make me certain that the murder has been done, then you are the pander to her dishonor and equally disloyal to me.*"

Pisanio said to himself, "What need do I have to draw my sword? The letter has cut her throat already. No, it is slander, whose edge is sharper than the sword, whose tongue is more poisonous than all the serpents of the Nile, whose breath rides on the swift winds and spreads lies over all the corners of the world. This viperous slander enters the lives of Kings, Queens, and lords, maidens, and matrons, and even creeps into the secrets of the grave."

He said out loud, "How are you, madam?"

Ignoring him, Imogen said, "False to his bed! What is it to be false and cheat on him? To lie awake in bed and to think about him? To weep from hour to hour because he is not there? If sleep restores our natural powers, does being false to his bed mean to wake up because of having a dream about danger to him? Does it mean to cry myself awake? Is that what it means to be false to his bed?"

"I am sorry, good lady!" Pisanio said.

Still ignoring Pisanio, but addressing people who were not present, Imogen said, "I false! I unfaithful to you? I cheat on you!

"Posthumus, your conscience should be a witness that I am true to you!

"Iachimo, you accused Posthumus of being unfaithful to me. You then looked like a villain, but now I think that your appearance is good enough.

"Some jay — some gaudy whore — of Italy whose mother was painting — makeup, not nature — has betrayed my husband. Poor me! I am stale, a garment out of fashion, but because I am richer than to hang on the walls, I must be ripped."

Imogen was comparing herself to a garment that was made of rich cloth but was out of fashion. Some old clothing was simply hung up on a wall of an old wardrobe and ignored (many of us have clothing hanging in our closets that we never wear), but unfashionable clothing made of a rich fabric would be disassembled so that the fabric could be reused.

Imogen said, "To pieces with me! Tear me to pieces! Oh, men's vows are traitors to women! Because of your turning away from me, husband, all men who put on a good appearance — say, of fidelity — shall be thought to be putting on a good appearance only so they can commit villainy. Their good appearance shall not be born — that is, come from their nature — but it will be worn as a bait for ladies."

"Good madam, listen to me," Pisanio said.

Ignoring him, Imogen continued, "Aeneas was false to Dido, Queen of Carthage. He seduced and then abandoned her. Because of him, the true and honest men of his time were thought to be false.

"The treacherous Greek named Sinon wept in order to convince the Trojans to take the Trojan Horse into Troy. Because of him, holy tears were mistrusted. Because of him, pity was diverted from those who very truly deserved pity.

"And so you, Posthumus, will lay the leaven on all proper men. You shall be the sour dough that spoils the good dough. Because of your great fall, the good and gallant shall be thought to be false and perjured."

Imogen then said to Pisanio, "Come, fellow, be honest. Do what your master ordered you to do: Kill me. When you see him, testify a little that I am obedient to him. Look! I draw the sword myself. Take it, and hit the innocent mansion of my love — my heart. Don't be afraid. It is empty of everything except grief. Your master, Posthumus, is not there. He indeed was once the riches stored in my heart. Do what he ordered you to do. Strike me with your sword. You may be valiant in a better cause, but now you seem to be a coward."

Pisanio threw away from him the sword that Imogen had placed in his hand and said, "Hence, vile instrument! You shall not damn my hand."

Imogen said to him, "Why, I must die; and if I do not die by your hand, you are no servant of your master's. Against self-slaughter — suicide — there is a prohibition so divine that it makes my weak hand cowardly. Come, here's my heart. Something is in front of it. Wait! Wait! We'll have no defense. My breast is as obedient as the scabbard; both are ready to admit the sword. What is here?"

She took some letters out of her bodice and said, "The scriptures of the 'loyal' Posthumus Leonatus, all turned to heresy!"

She threw Posthumus' letters to her on the ground and said, "Away, away, corrupters of my faith! You shall no more be a decorative cover over my heart. Thus may poor fools believe false teachers; although those who are betrayed feel the treason sharply, yet the traitor stands in worse case of woe.

"And you, Posthumus, who encouraged my disobedience against my father the King and who made me reject with contempt the suits of Princely fellows who wanted to marry me, shall hereafter find that it is no act of common occurrence, but a strain of rareness, for a Princess to marry a commoner, and I grieve myself to think that you shall grow sated with the harlot whom you now feed greedily on, and then you will be pained by remembering me."

She said to Pisanio, "Please, do your job. The lamb entreats the butcher to kill it. Where's your knife? You are too slow to do your master's bidding, when I desire it, too."

"Oh, gracious lady," Pisanio said, "since I received the command to do this business — to murder you — I have not slept one wink."

"Murder me, and then go to bed and sleep," Imogen replied.

"I'll stay awake until my eyeballs fall out before I kill you."

"Why then did you undertake to kill me?" Imogen asked. "Why have you traveled so many miles under a pretense? Why travel to this place? Why cause my journey and your own journey? Why cause our horses' labor? Why make me spend time persuading you to undertake this journey? Why help me to leave the court and be absent from and perturb it — the court where I never intend to return? Why have you gone so far, only to unbend your bow with its arrow after you have gone to your hunting place and see the deer, which you have chosen to kill, in front of you?"

"I did those things only to win time and find a way to not engage in such bad employment," Pisanio said. "It worked. While doing those things, I have thought of a course of action that we can take. Good lady, hear me patiently."

"Talk until your tongue is weary," Imogen replied. "Speak. I have heard that I am a strumpet; and my ear, wrongly struck and injured by that word, can take no greater wound because no wound is deeper. But speak."

"Then, madam, I have thought you would not go back to the court again."

"That is very likely," Imogen replied, "because you brought me here to kill me."

"That is not true," Pisanio said. "But if I am now being as wise as I am being honest, then my plan will prove to be a good one. It cannot be otherwise than that my master is being abused by being fed false information about you. Some villain, who is without equal in his art, has done this cursed injury to both you and your husband."

"Some Roman prostitute has done this," Imogen said.

"No, on my life," Pisanio said. "Your husband is not involved with an Italian prostitute. I'll tell your husband that you are dead, and I will send him some bloody sign of your death because he commanded that I should do so. You shall be missed at court, and that will well confirm that you are dead."

"Why, good fellow, what shall I do in the meantime? Where shall I stay? How shall I live? What pleasure can I have in my life, when I am dead to my husband?"

"If you'll go back to the court —" Pisanio began.

Imogen interrupted, "— no court, no father, and no more trouble with that harsh, high-ranking, simple nothing, that Cloten, whose lovesuit has been to me as fearful as a siege."

"If you will not live at court, then you cannot live in Britain."

"Where then can I live? Has Britain all the Sun that shines? Day, night, aren't they only in Britain? Our Britain seems to be a part of the world, but not in it. It seems to be a swan's nest in a great pool of water. Please think and tell me that people live outside of Britain."

"I am very glad that you are thinking of places other than Britain," Pisanio said. "The Roman ambassador, Caius Lucius, will come to Milford Haven tomorrow. Now, if you could wear a mind as dark as your fortune is, and if you could disguise that femininity that, if it were to appear as itself, as it should not because of danger to yourself, you should tread a course that is pretty and full of view — pleasing and full of good prospects. Yes, perhaps you could be near the residence of Posthumus — at least as near that although you may not see his actions, yet you could hear from other people truly what he is doing each hour."

Imogen, who understood that she must disguise that she is a woman and pretend to be a man in order to avoid the danger of rape, said, "Oh, for the means to do that! Although it would put my modesty in danger, it would not be the death of my modesty, and so I would undertake it."

"Well, then, here's the point," Pisanio said. "You must forget to be a woman. Change your noble right to command into a commoner's obedience. Change fear and fastidiousness — the handmaids of all women, or, more truly, the essence of woman, its pretty self — into a playful courage. Be ready to make joking insults, to make sharp answers, and to be as saucy and as quarrelsome as a weasel. Indeed, you must forget that rarest treasure of your cheek and darken its complexion by exposing it — this is hard for a woman who takes pride in her light complexion to do, but make your heart hard because you must do this! — to the greedy touch of the Sun, which kisses everyone, and you must neglect your laborious and dainty adornments that make you pretty, thereby making great Juno, the jealous wife of Jupiter, angry because she envies your beauty."

Imogen would have to wear men's clothing that would expose her face to the Sun and darken it through tanning. In her society, light complexions were valued, and upper-class women avoided exposing their faces to the Sun.

"Be brief in your speech," Imogen said. "I understand your plan, and I am already almost a man."

"First, make yourself look like one," Pisanio said. "I planned ahead, and I previously packed men's clothing for you in my cloak-bag — jacket, hat, breeches, all that is needed. With this clothing's assistance, and with your imitation of young men who are your age, you shall present yourself before noble Caius Lucius and ask to be employed by him. Tell him your skills and use your musical voice to persuade him to hire you — if he has an ear for music, he will without doubt welcome you because he's honorable and — better — he's very holy. As for your means abroad, you have me, rich, and I will never fail you either now or later."

Pisanio was not rich in money, but he was rich in qualities such as loyalty. As far as providing Imogen with food, subsequent events would show that he could not do that; for one thing, he needed to return to the court. Nevertheless, he remained loyal to her later, just as he was now. In addition, part of the job of certain servants is to hold the boss' bag of money. As Imogen's servant, he was holding on to Imogen's money for the time being. To a servant such as Pisanio, that amount of money would seem to be riches, indeed. When he left to return to the court, he would hand over to Imogen her money. In addition, he was planning, when needed, to visit her and take to her money from the court.

"You are all the comfort the gods will diet me with," Imogen said.

Imogen meant that she would have to rely on Pisanio; her words also subtly acknowledged that Pisanio might not be able to provide her with all the help she needed.

The gods do not always provide comfort and good diets. Imogen would not starve, but she would be hungry. But sometimes the gods allow bad things to happen before good things happen, just as a physician of the past could prescribe a course of fasting in an attempt to return a body to health and good appetite.

Fortunately, Imogen would receive help from people other than Pisanio.

She added, "Please, let's go. There's more to be planned and considered, but we'll sort all that out in the good time available to us. I have the courage to do what we have planned, and I will face it with the courage of a Prince. Let's go, please."

"Well, madam, we must make only a brief farewell, lest, once you are missed, I am suspected of conveying you away from the court. My noble mistress, here is a box of medicine. The Queen gave it to me. What's in it is precious: If you are sick at sea, or if you have an upset stomach on land, a little of this medicine will drive away your illness. Go into some thicket, and dress yourself like a man. May the gods take the best care of you!"

"Amen to that!" Imogen said. "I thank you."

King Cymbeline, the Queen, Cloten, and Caius Lucius were talking in a room of Cymbeline's palace. Some lords and attendants were also present.

Using the royal plural, Cymbeline said to Caius Lucius, "We have gone far enough, and so I say farewell to you."

"Thanks, royal sir," Caius Lucius replied. "My Emperor has written that I must leave, and I am very sorry that I must report to him that you are his enemy."

"Our subjects, sir, will not endure his yoke, and if I were to appear less patriotic that they are, then I would appear less than a King."

Caius Lucius replied, "So be it, sir. I request of you that you give me safe conduct — an escort — overland to Milford Haven."

He then said to the Queen, "Madam, may all joy befall your grace!"

The Queen replied, "And to you!"

"My lords, you are appointed for that duty," Cymbeline said to the lords present. "Give Caius Lucius safe conduct and escort him. Show him all honor that is due to him. Omit nothing."

Cymbeline then said, "So farewell, noble Lucius."

"Give me your hand, my lord."

"Receive it friendly," Cymbeline said, shaking hands with Caius Lucius.

Their hands separated, and Cymbeline said, "But from this time forth, this hand is the hand of your enemy."

"Sir, the upcoming war has yet to name the winner," Caius Lucius said. "Fare you well."

"Don't leave the worthy Lucius, my good lords," Cymbeline said, "until he has crossed the Severn River."

He said to Caius Lucius, "May happiness be a part of your life!"

Caius Lucius and the lords exited.

The Queen said to King Cymbeline, "He goes away from here frowning, but we have done the right thing in giving him cause to frown."

Cloten said, "It is for the best."

He then said to King Cymbeline, "Your valiant Britons want you to oppose the Romans."

"Lucius has already written to the Emperor what has happened here," Cymbeline said. "It is fitting for us therefore to immediately ensure that our chariots and our horsemen are in readiness. The troops that Lucius already has in France will soon be brought to full strength, and from France he will move to make war on Britain."

"This is not a time for sleeping," the Queen said. "Everything must be looked after speedily and strongly."

"Our expectation that war would occur has made us prepare early for it," Cymbeline said.

Using the royal plural, he said, "But, my gentle Queen, where is Imogen, our daughter? She did not appear before the Roman Caius Lucius, nor has she greeted us recently. To us, she seems more like a thing made of malice than a dutiful daughter. We have noticed it."

He ordered an attendant, "Tell her to appear now before us; we have been weak in allowing her to treat us this way."

An attendant left to summon Imogen to appear before her father.

The Queen said, "Royal sir, since the exile of Posthumus, her life has been most retired. She stays by herself most of the time. The cure for this, my lord, is time, which tames the strongest grief. I ask your majesty to not speak sharply to her: She's a lady who is so sensitive to rebukes that words are strokes, and strokes are death to her."

The attendant returned.

Cymbeline said to him, "Where is she, sir? How can her contemptible treatment of me be accounted for?"

"If it please you, sir, her rooms are all locked; and there's no answer given to the loudest noise we make," the attendant said.

The Queen said to Cymbeline, "My lord, when I last went to visit her, she asked me to excuse her keeping to herself, saying that she was ill and therefore was unable to greet you each day, as she was supposed to do. She wanted me to tell you this, but our great court business with Caius Lucius caused me to forget."

"Her doors are locked?" Cymbeline said. "No one has seen her recently? Heavens, may that which I fear prove not to have happened!"

He exited to go to his daughter's chambers. His attendants followed him.

The Queen said to Cloten, "Go, son, and follow the King."

Cloten replied, "That man of hers, Pisanio, her old servant, has not been seen for the past two days."

"Go, look after the King," the Queen said.

Cloten exited.

Alone, the Queen said to herself, "Pisanio serves as the advocate at court for Posthumus! He has a poisonous drug of mine; I pray that his absence from court is the result of his swallowing my drug because he believes that it is a most precious thing. But as for Imogen, where has she gone? Perhaps despair has seized her, or winged with the fervor of her love, she's flown to her desired Posthumus. She has gone either to death or to dishonor, and either one serves my purpose. With her out of the way, I can place the British crown on whose head I wish."

Cloten, who could possibly be the next King of Britain, returned.

The Queen said to him, "What is the news, my son?"

"It is certain that Imogen has fled. Go in and cheer up the King. He rages, and no one dares to come near him."

The Queen thought, *All the better. I hope that his rage kills him before the coming day!*

She exited.

Cloten said to himself about Imogen, "I love and hate her because she's beautiful and royal, and because she has all courtly accomplishments more exquisite than any other lady, ladies, woman. From everyone she has the best parts, and she, who is made of all the best parts blended together, surpasses everyone. I love her therefore, but her disdaining me and throwing her favors on the lowly born Posthumus so disgraces her judgment that what would otherwise be rare is suffocated, and because of that I hate her — indeed, because of that, I will be revenged upon her. For when fools shall —"

Cloten stopped talking because Pisanio entered the room.

Cloten said, "Who is here?"

Recognizing Pisanio, he said, "What are you plotting, sirrah?"

The word "sirrah" was used to address a male of lower social status than the speaker.

Cloten said to Pisanio, "Come here! Ah, you precious pander! Villain, where is your lady? Where is Imogen? Tell me quickly, or quickly I will send you to Hell so you can be with the fiends!"

"Oh, my good lord!"

"Where is your lady? Where is Imogen?" Cloten repeated. "Tell me, or by Jupiter I will not ask again. Secretive villain, I'll have this secret from your heart, or I'll rip your heart to find it. Is she with Posthumus? From Posthumus' many pounds of baseness even a part of an ounce of worth cannot be drawn."

"Alas, my lord," Pisanio said. "How can Imogen be with Posthumus? When was she discovered absent from the court? Posthumus is in Rome. She cannot have traveled that far so quickly to see him."

"Where is she then, sir?" Cloten asked. "Come nearer. No further faltering. Tell me exactly what has become of her."

"Oh, my all-worthy lord!"

"All-worthy villain!" Cloten replied. "Reveal to me where your mistress is at once, using your next word. Let me hear no more of 'worthy lord!' Speak, or your silence will result immediately in your condemnation and your death."

"Then, sir, this letter is the history of my knowledge concerning her flight," Pisanio said.

He held up the letter in which Posthumus had told Imogen to meet him at Milford Haven. In doing this, he was not betraying Imogen because he thought that she had left the region.

Cloten said, "Let me see the letter. I will pursue Imogen even all the way to the throne of Caesar Augustus."

He took it and began to read it.

Pisanio thought, *I had to do this, or perish. But Imogen is far enough away from Milford Haven to be safe, and what Cloten learns by reading this letter may prove to be his travail and not her danger.*

Reading the letter, Cloten grunted.

Pisanio thought, *I'll write to my lord, Posthumus, that she's dead. Oh, Imogen, safe may you wander, and safe return again!*

"Sirrah, is this letter true?"

"Sir, I think it is."

"It is Posthumus' handwriting; I recognize it," Cloten said. "Sirrah, if you wish not to be a villain, but instead to do me true service, undertake with a serious industry those tasks in which I should have reason to use you; that is, whatever villainy I order you to do, perform it immediately and truly — I wish to think that you are an honest man. If you prove to serve me faithfully, you will neither want my means for your relief nor my voice for your advancement. You will be richly rewarded for your service."

"Good, my good lord," Pisanio replied.

"Will you serve me? Patiently and steadfastly you have stuck to the bare fortune of that beggar Posthumus, and so you cannot, in the course of gratitude, but be a diligent follower of mine. Posthumus could not reward you well for your service, but I can. Will you serve me?"

"Sir, I will."

"Give me your hand," Cloten said. "Here's my bag of money for you to take care of. Do you have any of your recent master's — Posthumus' — garments in your possession?"

"I have, my lord, at my lodging, the same suit of clothing that Posthumus wore when he took leave of my lady and mistress: Imogen."

This is unlikely. Posthumus was wearing the clothing when he left, so how could Pisanio have possession of them? Pisanio was engaging in an act of rebellion against Cloten: He was lying to him.

"The first service you will do me is to fetch that suit of clothing and bring it here," Cloten said. "Let it be your first service; go."

"I shall, my lord," Pisanio said as he exited.

"Posthumus and Imogen will meet at Milford Haven!" Cloten said. "I forgot to ask Pisanio one thing: I'll remember it soon.

"At Milford Haven, you villain Posthumus, I will kill you. I wish these garments of yours were here now. Imogen said once — the bitterness of it I now belch from my heart — that she held the garment of Posthumus in more respect than my noble and natural person even with the adornment of my qualities. While wearing Posthumus' clothing on my back, I will rape her. First I will kill him in front of her. That way, she will witness my valor, which will then be a torment to her because of her contempt of me. The insults I will say will end when he lies dead on the ground, and when my lust has dined on her body — which, as I say, to vex her I will rape her while I wear the clothes that she so praised — then I'll beat her back to the court, kicking her home again. She has despised me with delight, and I'll be merry in my revenge."

Pisanio had come back early enough to hear Cloten's plan to rape Imogen. Cloten had not been aware of Pisanio's presence because Pisanio had stopped a short distance away and had been quiet, but now Pisanio walked toward him, carrying a suit of clothing.

"Are those Posthumus' clothes?" Cloten asked.

"Yes, my noble lord."

Remembering what he had forgotten to ask Pisanio previously, Cloten asked, "How long has it been since Imogen went to Milford Haven?"

"She can scarcely have arrived there yet," Pisanio answered.

This was another lie. Pisanio had had time to return to the court after leaving Imogen near Milford Haven.

"Take this apparel to my chamber; that is the second thing that I have commanded you to do. The third is that you will be a voluntary mute about my plan — don't make me cut off your tongue! Don't tell anyone what I am planning to do. Do your duty to me, and true advancement shall come to you. My revenge is now at Milford Haven. I wish that I had wings to follow it! Come, and serve me faithfully and truly."

Cloten exited.

Pisanio said to himself, "You order me to do things that will be to my loss because if I am true to you, then I am false, which I will never be, to him — Posthumus — who is most true. To Milford Haven you will go, and you will not find her — Imogen — whom you are pursuing! Flow, flow, you Heavenly blessings, on her! May this fool's speed be thwarted by slowness; may hard work be his reward!"

Imogen, wearing the clothing of a young man, stood in front of Belarius' (Morgan's) cave in Wales.

She said to herself, "I see a man's life is a tedious one. I have attired myself in men's clothing, and I have tired myself by walking, and for the past two nights I have made the ground my bed. I should be sick, but my determination to be near my husband helps me.

"Milford Haven, when Pisanio showed you to me from the mountaintop, you were within sight. By Jove, I think places where help can be found flee from the wretched — such people, I mean, who deserve to be relieved from their distress. Two beggars told me that I could not miss my way. Will poor folks lie in order to get alms, although they know that their afflictions are a punishment or test sent from Heaven? Yes, and it is no wonder then that beggars lie when rich people will scarcely tell the truth. To sin when one is prosperous is worse than to lie because of need, and falsehood is worse in Kings than it is in beggars.

"My dear husband: Posthumus! You are one of the false ones! Now that I am thinking about you, my hunger's gone; but just a moment before, I was ready to sink to the ground because of lack of food.

"But what is this? Here is a path to a cave: It is some stronghold for savages. It would be best if I did not call to whoever is here. I dare not call, yet famine, before it wholly overthrows a person's nature, makes that nature valiant and courageous. Plenty and peace breed cowards: hardship is always the mother of courage.

"Hey! Who's here? If you are anyone who is civilized, speak; if savage, act — take my money and life or lend me aid. Hey! No answer? Then I'll enter.

"I had best draw my sword. If my enemy fears a sword like I do, he'll scarcely look on it. May the good Heavens give me such a foe!"

She entered the cave.

Belarius (Morgan), Guiderius (Polydore) and Arviragus (Cadwal) arrived, carrying the game they had hunted.

Belarius (Morgan) said, "You, Polydore, have proved to be the best hunter and so you are the master of the feast. Cadwal and I will play the cook and servant; that is the agreement we made. The sweat of industry would dry and die, except for the end it works to. We would not do the hard work of hunting except for the necessity of feeding ourselves. Come; our stomachs will make plain and simple food savory and delicious. A weary person can snore while lying upon flinty ground, while a lazy and slothful person finds a down pillow hard. Now may peace be here, poor cave and home, that we left all alone!"

"I am thoroughly weary," Guiderius (Polydore) said.

"I am weak with toil, yet strong in appetite," Arviragus (Cadwal) said.

"There is cold food in the cave," Guiderius (Polydore) said. "We'll nibble on that while what we have killed is being cooked."

Belarius (Morgan) looked into the cave and said to the others, "Stay outside; do not come in. Except that it eats our food, I would think here is a creature of enchantment."

"What's the matter, sir?" Guiderius (Polydore) asked.

"By Jupiter, I see an angel!" Belarius (Morgan) said. "Or, if not, an earthly paragon! Behold divineness no elder than a boy!"

Imogen came out of the cave and said, "Good masters, don't hurt me. Before I entered the cave here, I called, and I intended to have begged or bought what I have taken. Truly, I have stolen nothing, nor would I, even though I had found gold strewn on the floor."

She held out some money and said, "Here's money for my food. I would have left it on the table as soon as I had finished my meal, and parted with prayers for the provider."

Guiderius (Polydore) said, "Money, youth?"

Arviragus (Cadwal) said, "All gold and silver should turn to dirt! Gold and silver are not thought to be better than dirt except by those who worship dirty, repulsive gods!"

Imogen said, "I see you're angry. Know, if you kill me for my fault, I would have died had I not committed the fault of eating your food without first getting permission."

"Where are you going?" Belarius (Morgan) asked her.

"To Milford Haven."

"What's your name?"

"Fidele, sir."

Fidele is French for "the faithful one."

Imogen (Fidele) continued, "I have a relative who is bound for Italy; he embarked at Milford Haven. I was going to him, when almost exhausted with hunger, I committed this offence."

"Please, fair youth," Belarius (Morgan) said. "Don't think that we are brutes, and don't judge our good minds by this rude cave we live in. It is good that you encountered us! It is almost night. You shall have better entertainment before you depart, and we will thank you to stay and eat our food."

He then said, "Boys, make him welcome."

Guiderius (Polydore) said, "Were you a woman, youth, I would woo you hard so I could be your legal bridegroom. I would bid for you as if I intended definitely to buy you."

Arviragus (Cadwal) said, "I am glad that he is a man. I'll love him as I love my brother, and such a welcome as I would give to my brother after a long absence, I give to you, Fidele. You are very welcome here! Be cheerful because you have fallen among friends."

Imogen (Fidele) thought, *Among friends, as long as we are brothers. I wonder if you would still be friends if you knew that I am a woman. Being a lone woman among strange men is dangerous. I wish that you really were my brothers — my father's sons. If you were my father's sons, then I would not be heir to my father's kingdom, and so I would be more equal to you, Posthumus, and I would be much more likely to be allowed to be married to you.*

Imogen (Fidele) did not know it, but these two young men — Guiderius (Polydore) and Arviragus (Cadwal) — really were her brothers, whom Belarius had kidnapped when they were very young.

Belarius (Morgan) said, "He wrings his hands because of some distress."

"I wish that I could free him of that distress!" Guiderius (Polydore) said.

"As do I," Arviragus (Cadwal) said, whatever that distress is, and whatever pain it would cost me, and whatever danger it would put me in. Gods!"

"Listen to me, boys," Belarius (Morgan) said to Guiderius (Polydore) and Arviragus (Cadwal).

He whispered to them.

Imogen (Fidele) thought, *Great men who had a court no bigger than this cave, who served themselves instead of having others serve them, and who had the virtue that their own conscience ratified in them — disregarding that worthless gift of the adulation of fickle multitudes of people — could not surpass these two young men. Pardon me, gods! I would change my sex to be companions with them, since Leonatus is false to me.*

Belarius (Morgan) said to his two "sons," "It shall be done. Boys, we'll go prepare our game for cooking."

He said to Imogen (Fidele), "Fair youth, come in. Conversation is difficult to make when we are hungry; when we have eaten, we'll politely ask you to tell your story, as much as you are willing to tell of it."

"Please, come near," Guiderius (Polydore) said to Imogen (Fidele).

Arviragus (Cadwal) said, "The night to the owl and the morning to the lark are less welcome than you are to us."

"Thanks, sir," Imogen (Fidele) replied.

"Please, come near," Arviragus (Cadwal) said to her.

— 3.7 —

Two Senators and some Tribunes met in a public place in Rome.

The first Senator said, "This is the substance of the Emperor's command: That since the common men are now in action fighting against the Pannonians in Hungary and the Dalmatians on the Adriatic Sea, and since the legions now in France are too weak to undertake our wars against the rebelling Britons, that we summon the gentry to go to war against the Britons. Caesar Augustus makes Caius Lucius Proconsul, and he delegates to you the Tribunes his complete authority to raise this immediate levy of soldiers. Long live Caesar!"

"Is Caius Lucius the general of the armed forces?" the first Tribune asked.

"Yes," the second Senator said.

"Is he still in France?" the first Tribune asked.

The first Senator replied, "He is with those legions of soldiers that I have spoken of, whereunto your levy of soldiers must be the reinforcements. The words of your commission will stipulate the numbers of the soldiers you will draft and the time they will be dispatched to France."

"We will do our duty," the first Tribune said.

CHAPTER 4
— 4.1 —

Cloten, wearing Posthumus' clothing, stood near Belarius' (Morgan's) cave.

Alone, he said to himself, "I am near the place where Posthumus and Imogen should meet, if Pisanio has mapped the place truly and correctly. How fittingly his garments serve me! Why shouldn't his mistress, who was made by Him — God — Who made the tailor, be fitting for me, too? I fit in Posthumus' clothing, so why shouldn't I fit in his wife? Pardon the sexual puns, but it is said a woman's fitness — readiness for a sexual workout — comes by fits and starts. Therein I must play the skilled workman and make sure that I fit in her.

"I dare to say this to myself — for it is not vainglorious for a man and his mirror to confer privately in his own bedchamber — I mean, the lines of my body are as well drawn as those of Posthumus' body. I am no less young, I am stronger, I am not beneath him in fortunes, I am superior to him in having the advantage of social connections, I am above him in birth, I am equally experienced as him in general military services, and I am more remarkable in single combat and duels.

"Yet this stubborn and blind thing — Imogen — loves him instead of me. What a thing human nature is!

"Posthumus, your head, which now is growing upon your shoulders, shall within this hour be cut off. Your wife shall be raped, your garments shall be cut to pieces before her face, and when all this is done, I will kick her home to her father. He may perhaps be a little angry for my very rough treatment of your wife, who is his daughter, but my mother, who has the power to change his testiness, shall turn all his criticisms of me into commendations of me.

"My horse is tied up safely. Out, sword, because I will use you for a grievous purpose! Fortune, put Posthumus and Imogen into my hands! This place matches the exact description of their meeting place, and that fellow Pisanio does not dare to deceive me."

Belarius (Morgan) came out of the cave. With him were Guiderius (Polydore), Arviragus (Cadwal), and Imogen (Fidele). Everyone still thought that Imogen was the young man Fidele.

Belarius (Morgan) said to Imogen (Fidele), "You are not well. Remain here in the cave, and we'll come to you after hunting."

Arviragus (Cadwal) said to her, "Brother, stay here. Are we not brothers?"

Not feeling well because of the hardships she had gone through, Imogen (Fidele) said, "Although both men are made from clay, and although both turn to dust when they die, yet they can differ in social class. But man and man should be brothers."

Guiderius (Polydore) said to Belarius (Morgan) and Arviragus (Cadwal), "You two go and hunt. I'll stay with him."

"I am not sick, although I am not well," Imogen (Fidele) said. "I am not so citified a pampered child that I seem ready to die before I am sick. Please, leave me here, alone. Stick to your normal daily activities. Breaking a routine upsets everything. I am ill, but your being beside me cannot heal me; society is no comfort to one who is not sociable. I am not very sick, since I can talk reasonably about it — I am not delirious. Please, trust me to be alone here. I'll rob no one but myself; and let me die if I steal from one who is that poor. I will deserve to die since I am such a poor thief."

Guiderius (Polydore) said to her, "I love you; I have said it. I love you as much and as deeply as I love my father."

"What!" Belarius (Morgan) said, surprised.

"Even if it is a sin to say so, I share my good brother's fault," Arviragus (Cadwal) said. "I don't know why I love this youth, and I have heard you say that love is without reason. If a bier were at the door, and I was asked who should die, I would say, 'My father, not this youth.'"

Belarius (Morgan) marveled at how much his "sons" loved this young man whom they had just recently met. Such love must come from the young man's good and noble character, which must be like the good and noble character — a result of their noble heritage — of his "sons." It was likely that the young man also had a noble heritage.

He thought, *Oh, noble strain! Oh, worthiness of nature! Oh, breed of greatness! Cowards father cowards and base things sire base things. Nature has meal and bran, contempt and grace. I'm not these two boys' biological father; but whoever this Fidele is, it is a miracle that these two boys love him more than they love me.*

He said out loud, "It is the ninth hour of the morning."

"Brother, farewell," Arviragus (Cadwal) said.

"I wish you good hunting," Imogen (Fidele) said.

"I wish you health," Arviragus (Cadwal) replied.

He said to Belarius (Morgan), "I am ready, sir."

These are kind creatures, Imogen thought. *By the gods, what lies I have heard! Our courtiers say everyone is savage except those who are at court. Experience, you have disproved what they say! The imperious seas breed monsters, but the poor tributary rivers breed no monsters although they breed as good fish for our dishes as the imperious seas do. I am still sick; I am heartsick. Pisanio, I'll now taste of the drug that you gave me.*

She swallowed some of the drug that Pisanio had given to her; it was the same drug that the Queen had given to Pisanio.

The three men talked quietly together, away from Imogen.

Guiderius (Polydore) said about Imogen (Fidele), "I could not get him to say much about himself. He said he was well born, but unfortunate; he was afflicted by dishonorable people, but he himself was still honest and honorable."

"He said the same thing to me," Arviragus (Cadwal) said, "but he added that later I might learn more."

"To the field, to the field!" Belarius (Morgan) said. "It is time to hunt."

He said to Imogen (Fidele), "We'll leave you for awhile. Go in the cave and rest."

"We'll not be away for long," Arviragus (Cadwal) said.

"Please, don't be sick," Belarius (Morgan) said to her, "because you must manage our household."

"Whether I am well or ill, I am bound to you," Imogen (Fidele) said.

"And shall be forever," Belarius (Morgan) replied.

She had used the word "bound" to mean "obliged," but he had used it to mean "bound by mutual affection."

Imogen (Fidele) went into the cave.

Belarius (Morgan) then said, "This youth, however distressed he is, appears to have had good ancestors."

"How like an angel he sings!" Arviragus (Cadwal) marveled.

"And his elegant cookery!" Guiderius (Polydore) said. "He cut our roots into shapes and letters, and he seasoned our broths just as if the goddess Juno — who would expect fine food — had been sick and he was her dietician."

"Nobly he links a smile with a sigh, as if the sigh was what it was because it was not such a smile; the smile is mocking the sigh because it would fly from so divine a temple and mingle with winds that sailors rail at," Arviragus (Cadwal) said.

"I noticed that grief and patience, both of which are rooted in him, mingle their roots together," Guiderius (Polydore) said. "He is sorrowful, but he manages his sorrow well."

"May the root of patience grow in him," Arviragus (Cadwal) said. "And may grief — the dying and destructive root of the stinking elder tree, from which Judas hanged himself — untwine itself from the growing vine of patience!"

"It is now fully morning," Belarius (Morgan) said. "Come, let's go and hunt!"

He saw something move and said quietly to his "sons," "Who's there?"

Cloten came into view, but he did not see the three men immediately.

Cloten said to himself, "I cannot find those renegades; that villain has fooled me. I am faint."

Belarius (Morgan) said quietly, "'Those renegades!' Doesn't he mean us? I somewhat know him: He is Cloten, the son of the Queen. I fear some ambush. I have not seen him for many years, and yet I know it is he. We are regarded as outlaws! Run!"

Guiderius (Polydore) replied, "He is only one man; he is alone. You and my brother go and search to see which other people are near. Please, go. Let me alone with him. I will deal with him."

Belarius (Morgan) and Arviragus (Cadwal) exited.

Cloten saw them leaving and called, "Wait! Who are you two who are running away from me like this? Are you some villainous criminals who live in the mountains? I have heard of such."

He asked Guiderius (Polydore), "What slave are you?"

The word "slave" was an insult that meant "villain."

"The most slavish thing I can ever do is to let you insult me without my giving you a blow in return," Guiderius (Polydore) replied.

Cloten replied, "You are a robber, a law-breaker, a villain. Surrender, thief."

"To whom? To you? Who are you? Don't I have an arm as big as your arm? A heart as big? Your words, I grant, are bigger, for I don't wear my dagger in my mouth. Say who you are. Explain why I should surrender to you."

"You base villain, don't you realize who I am by looking at the sort of clothing I am wearing?"

"No, I don't know who you are," Guiderius (Polydore) said. "Nor, rascal, do I know who your tailor is, although he must be your grandfather. He made those clothes, and you think that your clothes make you, and so your tailor is your grandfather."

"You worthless rascal," Cloten said, "My tailor did not make these clothes."

Cloten was wearing Posthumus' clothing.

"Leave, then, and thank the man who gave them to you. You are some fool, and so I am loath to beat you."

"You insulting thief, hear what my name is, and tremble."

"What's your name?"

"Cloten, you villain."

"If Cloten, you double villain, is your name, I cannot tremble at it. If your name were Toad, or Adder, or Spider, all of which are venomous creatures, it would make a bigger impression on me."

"To your further fear — no, to your complete confusion, you should know that I am the Queen's son."

"I am sorry that you are the son of the Queen; you don't seem to be worthy of your high birth."

"Aren't you afraid now?" Cloten asked.

"I fear those whom I revere, the wise. I laugh at fools — I do not fear them."

"Now you shall die," Cloten said. "After I have slain you with my own hand, I'll follow those who just now fled from here, and on the gates of Lud's town I will display your heads. Surrender, hillbilly mountaineer."

They exited, fighting.

Belarius (Morgan) met Arviragus (Cadwal) and asked, "Did you see any people nearby?"

"None in the world. You mistook the identity of this man, I am sure."

"Let me think," Belarius (Morgan) said. "It has been a long time since I saw him, but time has not blurred the facial features that he had the last time I saw him. Also, the hesitations in his speech, followed by bursts of speaking, are exactly the same as they were. I am absolutely sure that this man is really Cloten."

"We left my brother and Cloten in this place. I hope that my brother makes short work of him. You say that Cloten is so savage and cruel."

Belarius (Morgan) replied, "Cloten roars as if he is a terror; he frightens people with his bluster. Your brother is young; he is scarcely a man. Because of his youth, he has no experience of such blustery roaring 'terrors' as Cloten. I hope that your brother is not afraid of him, as he may be if he mistakes the bluster of threats for the reality of danger. Defective judgment about a man's character can cause that man to be feared. But, look, your brother is coming."

Carrying Cloten's head, Guiderius (Polydore) walked over to them and said, "This Cloten was a fool. His head is an empty purse with no money in it. Hercules performed many almost impossible labors, but even he would be unable to knock out Cloten's brains, because Cloten had none. Yet if I had not cut off his head, the fool would be carrying my head instead of me carrying his head."

Belarius (Morgan), who was aware of the seriousness of killing the son of the Queen, said, "What have you done!"

"I know exactly what I have done. I have cut off the head of Cloten, son of the Queen, according to his own report; he called me 'traitor' and 'mountaineer,' and he swore that with his own unassisted hand he would capture us and displace our heads from where — thank the gods! — they grow, and display them in Lud's town."

"We are all undone, ruined, and destroyed," Belarius (Morgan) said.

"Why, worthy father, what have we to lose, except that which he swore to take, our lives?" Guiderius (Polydore) said. "The law does not protect us, so why then should we be so meek and spineless that we let an arrogant piece of flesh threaten us and play judge and executioner all by himself? Should we do that because we fear the law?"

He paused and then asked, "Did you discover any other men in this area?"

Belarius (Morgan) replied, "We have not laid an eye on a single soul, but level-headed reason tells me that he must have some attendants. His mood was very changeable, yes, and he changed from one bad thing to another that was worse; however, not frenzy, not even absolute madness could have so far possessed him that he would come here alone. Perhaps at court news is spread that such as we live in caves here, hunt here, are outlaws here, and in time may make some stronger fighting force; if he heard that news, then it is like him to break out in speech and swear that he would capture us and fetch us into the court, yet it is not probable that he would come alone. He is unlikely to want to come alone, and the others at court are unlikely to allow him to come alone, and so we have good grounds to fear that other men are near us. Like a scorpion, this body of men has a tail more perilous than the head. Cloten was not much of a danger, but the men he must have brought with him will be more dangerous than he."

"Let what is ordained come just as the gods foretell it," Arviragus (Cadwal) said. "However, my brother has done well."

"I was not in the mood to hunt today," Belarius (Morgan) said. "The boy Fidele's sickness made my walk away from the cave seem long."

Guiderius (Polydore) said, "With Cloten's own sword, which he waved against my throat, I have taken his head away from him. I'll throw it into the creek behind our cave and let it go to the sea, where it will tell the fishes he's the Queen's son, Cloten. That's all I care about him."

Guiderius (Polydore) exited.

"I am afraid that Cloten's death will be revenged," Belarius (Morgan) said. "I wish, Polydore, you had not killed him, although valor becomes you well enough."

"I wish that I had killed him, as long as the revenge pursued only me!" Arviragus (Cadwal) said. "Polydore, I love you like the brother you are, but I am very envious of you because you have robbed me of this deed. I wish that avengers, whom we could fight with the strength we have, would thoroughly seek us and force us to fight them."

"Well, it is done," Belarius (Morgan) said. "Cloten is dead. We'll hunt no more today, nor will we seek danger where there's no profit in doing so. Please, go to our cave. You and Fidele be the cooks today; I'll stay here until impulsive Polydore returns, and I'll bring him home to dinner soon."

"Poor sick Fidele! To get his color back to him, I'd willingly make a parish full of Clotens bleed, and I would praise myself for acting charitably."

Arviragus (Cadwal) exited.

Belarius (Morgan) said to himself, "Oh, goddess, you divine Nature, how you proclaim yourself in these two Princely boys! They are as gentle as zephyrs blowing below the violets, not wagging their sweet heads; and yet they are as rough, once their royal blood is heated, as the rudest wind that takes the top of a mountain pine and makes it stoop to the valley. It is wonderful that an invisible, unseen instinct should shape them to act royally and honorably without having been taught to act that way, and to act civilly without seeing models of such behavior. Valor grows wild in them, but it yields a crop as if it had been sowed. They act like Princes without having been taught how to act like Princes.

"Yet it's still a mystery what Cloten's being here signifies to us, and what his death will bring us."

Guiderius (Polydore) came back and said, "Where's my brother? I have sent Cloten's idiot head down the stream on an embassy to his mother. His body is being held hostage until his head's return."

Solemn music began to play.

"My ingenious musical instrument!" Belarius (Morgan) said. "Listen, Polydore, it is playing! But why is Cadwal now making it play? Listen!"

He was referring to a musical instrument that he had built to be played only on important solemn occasions.

"Is he at home?"

"He went there just now."

Guiderius (Polydore) said, "What does he mean by starting up the musical instrument? It has not played since the death of my very dear mother. All solemn things, including solemn music, should correspond to solemn events. What is the matter? Triumphs to celebrate nothing and laments over trifles are fun for apes and grief for boys. Is Cadwal mad? Is he playing this music to grieve over the death of Cloten?"

Belarius (Morgan) said, "Look, here he comes. We have been blaming him for playing this music, but he carries the dire reason for this solemn music in his arms."

Arviragus (Cadwal), carrying the stiff body of Imogen (Fidele) in his arms, walked over to them.

He said, "The bird is dead that we have made so much about. I would rather have skipped from sixteen years of age to sixty, to have turned my vigorous and youthful leaping-time into a time in which I need a crutch, than to have seen this."

"Oh, sweetest, fairest lily!" Guiderius (Polydore) said. "My brother wears you like a flower that is not even one-half as good as when you were still alive and growing."

Arviragus (Cadwal) placed the body on the ground.

"Melancholy!" Belarius (Morgan) said. "Whoever yet could sound your bottom as if you were a river and plumb your depths? Whoever could find the ooze at the bottom, to show what coast your sluggish small trading boat might most easily harbor in? You blessed thing! Jove knows what man you might have been when you grew up; but I know that you, a very rare boy, died of melancholy."

He said to Arviragus (Cadwal), "How was he when you found him?"

"Stiff, as you see him now, and smiling like he is now, as if some fly had tickled him in his slumber, not as if he was laughing at death's dart. His right cheek was resting on a cushion."

"Where was he?" Guiderius (Polydore) asked.

"On the floor. His arms were crossed against his chest. I thought he slept, and took off my hobnailed boots, whose coarseness made my steps too loud."

"Why, he is only sleeping," Guiderius (Polydore) said. "If he is dead and gone, he'll make his grave into a bed. Female fairies will stay near his tomb —"

He turned to the body of Imogen (Fidele) and said, "— and worms will not come to you."

Arviragus (Cadwal) said, "With the fairest flowers while summer lasts and I live here, Fidele, I'll sweeten your sad grave. You shall not lack the flower that's like your face, pale primrose, nor shall you lack the colored-like-a-clear-sky bluebell, which is the same color as your veins, nor shall you lack the leaf of eglantine, which I do not mean to slander when I say that it does not smell sweeter than your breath. The robin, with its charitable bill — the bill that greatly shames those rich heirs who allow their fathers to lie without a monument! — will bring your body all these flowers, and furred moss besides, when in winter there are no flowers, to cover your corpse."

"Please, finish," the practical Guiderius (Polydore) said, "and do not play with womanish words in that which is so serious. Let us bury him, and not defer with admiration and wonder what is now a due debt. Let's carry his body to the grave."

"Where shall we bury him?" Arviragus (Cadwal) asked.

"By good Euriphile, our mother."

"Let's do it," Arviragus (Cadwal) said, "and let us, Polydore, though now our voices have the broken-voice quality of young men, sing as we bury him, as once we buried our mother. We will sing the same notes and words, except that we are singing for Fidele and not for Euriphile."

"Cadwal, I cannot sing," Guiderius (Polydore) said. "I'll weep and say the words with you. Sorrowful notes that are out of tune are worse than priests and oracles who lie."

"We'll speak the words, then."

Belarius (Morgan) said, "Great griefs, I see, cure lesser griefs because Cloten is quite forgotten. He was a Queen's son, boys, and although he came to us as our enemy, remember that he paid for that. Although the lowly and the mighty, rotting together, have one dust, yet respectful esteem, that angel of the world, makes a distinction of place between highly born and lowly born. Our foe was Princely, and although you took his life, because he was our foe, yet we should bury him as a Prince should be buried."

Guiderius (Polydore) said to Belarius (Morgan), "Please, fetch Cloten's body here. Thersites' body is as good as Great Ajax' body, when neither is alive."

Great Ajax was a great Greek warrior in the Trojan War, second only to Achilles. Thersites, a common Greek soldier, was ugly and quarrelsome.

"If you'll go and fetch him," Arviragus (Cadwal) said, "we'll say our song while you are gone. Brother, begin."

Belarius (Morgan) exited to get Cloten's body.

"No, Cadwal," Guiderius (Polydore) said. "The body is not placed correctly. We must lay his head to the east; my father has a reason for it."

They were not Christian; they worshipped the Sun.

"That is true," Arviragus (Cadwal) said.

"Come on then, and let's move him."

They moved the body, and Arviragus (Cadwal) said, "Good. Begin."

Guiderius (Polydore) began the song:

"Fear no more the heat of the Sun,

"Nor the furious winter's rages.

"You your worldly task have done,

"Home have you gone, and taken your wages.

"Golden lads and girls all must,

"Like chimney sweepers, come to dust."

Arviragus (Cadwal) next took up the song:

"Fear no more the frown of the great;

"You are past the tyrant's stroke.

"Care no more to clothe and eat;

"To you the reed is the same as the oak.

"The scepter, learning, physic, must

[*"The scepter, learning, physic"* referred to Kings and worldly power, scholars and education, and doctors and medicine.]

"All endure death, and come to dust."

Guiderius (Polydore) spoke next:

"Fear no more the lightning flash,"

Then Arviragus (Cadwal) spoke:

"Nor the all-dreaded thunderstone."

[The thunderstone was a lightning bolt, which people of that time thought came down with stones from the sky.]

Guiderius (Polydore):

"Fear not slander, censure rash;"

Arviragus (Cadwal):

"You have finished joy and moan."

Both together:

"All lovers young, all lovers must

"Do like you, and come to dust."

Guiderius (Polydore):

"May no exorciser [spirit-raiser] harm you!"

Arviragus (Cadwal):

"Nor no witchcraft charm you!"
Guiderius (Polydore):
"Ghost unlaid forbear you!"
["May no restless ghost trouble you!"]
Arviragus (Cadwal):
"May nothing ill come near you!"
Both together:
"Quiet end of life have;
"And renowned be your grave!"
Belarius (Morgan) returned, carrying the headless body of Cloten.

Guiderius (Polydore) said, "We have done our obsequies. Come, lay him down."

"Here are a few flowers," Belarius (Morgan) said, "but at about midnight, there will be more. The herbs that have on them the cold dew of the night are the best and fittest to be strewn on graves. Put these flowers on the front of their bodies."

He said to the two bodies, "You were like flowers, but now you are withered. So shall be these little herbs, which we now strew upon you."

He then said to his two "sons": "Come on, let's go. Away from them, we'll get upon our knees and pray. The ground that gave them first has them again. Their pleasures here in the living world are past, and so is their pain."

They exited.

Imogen (Fidele) had not taken poison, but only a drug that made her sleep deeply for a while.

She woke up next to the headless Cloten, who was wearing her husband's clothes.

Still dreaming and thinking that she was asking for directions to Milford Haven, she said, "Yes, sir, to Milford Haven; which is the way? ... I thank you. ... By yonder bush? ... Please, how much farther is it? ... God, have pity! Can it really be six more miles? ... I have walked all night. Indeed, I'll lie down and sleep for a while."

She then fully woke up, felt Cloten's body next to her, and said, "But, wait! I need no bedfellow!"

She looked at Cloten's body and said, "Oh, gods and goddesses! These flowers are like the pleasures of the world; this bloody man is like the sorrow in it. I hope I am dreaming because I also dreamt that I was a cave-dweller and a cook to honest men, but that is not so — it was but an arrow of nothing, shot at nothing, an arrow that the brain makes of fumes. Our own eyes are sometimes like our judgments, blind."

People of the time thought that fumes rising from the body would go to the brain and cause dreams.

She continued, "Truly, I tremble stiff with fear, but if there is yet left in Heaven a drop of pity as small as a wren's eye, feared gods, give me a part of it! The dream is still here. Even when I awake, it is outside me, as it was within me; it is not imagined — it is felt."

Because Cloten was dressed in the clothing of her husband, Imogen (Fidele) thought that it was her husband lying dead beside her.

She continued, "A headless man! The garments of Posthumus! I know the shape of his leg. This is his hand. This is his foot like that of the messenger god Mercury. This is his thigh like that of Mars, the god of war. These are the muscles of Hercules, but his face that is like that of Jupiter ... is there murder in Heaven? ... what! ... his face is gone!

"Pisanio, may all the curses that insane Hecuba gave the Greeks, and my curses, also, be shot at you!"

Following the fall of Troy, its Queen, Hecuba, became insane as a result of grief. She cursed the Greeks for the deaths they had inflicted on members of her family.

Imogen (Fidele) continued, "Pisanio, you must have conspired with that lawless devil, Cloten, and have here killed my husband. To write and to read are from now on treacherous! Pisanio has with his forged letters — damned Pisanio — from this most splendid vessel of the world struck off the top of the main mast! Posthumus! I mourn! Where is your head? Where is it? Pisanio might have killed you by striking you in the heart, and left you your head.

"How could this come to be? Pisanio? He and Cloten have done this! Cloten's malice and Pisanio's greed have laid this woeful corpse here. Oh, it is clear, clear! The drug Pisanio gave me, which he said was precious and medicinal to me, have I not found it murderous to the senses? That completely confirms it. This is Pisanio's deed, as well as Cloten's."

She smeared her cheeks with blood while saying to the corpse, "Give color to my pale cheek with your blood, so that we may seem all the more horrid to those who chance to find us. Oh, my lord, my lord!"

She lay on the corpse.

General Caius Lucius, a Roman Captain, some other officers, and a soothsayer arrived on the scene, but they did not immediately notice Imogen (Fidele) and the headless corpse. They were busy discussing military preparations.

The Captain said to Caius Lucius, "In addition to those forces, the legions garrisoned in France, following your orders, have crossed the sea, and are awaiting you here at Milford Haven with your ships. They are all ready."

Caius Lucius asked, "What forces are coming from Rome?"

The Captain replied, "The Senate has stirred up the inhabitants and gentlemen of Italy, who are very willing spirits and who promise to provide noble service, and they are coming here under the command of bold Iachimo, the brother of the Duke of Siena."

"When do you expect them?"

"I expect them to arrive with the next favorable wind."

"This state of preparedness makes our hopes of success fair," Caius Lucius said. "Command our present numbers to be mustered; order the captains to do it."

He then asked the soothsayer, "Now, sir, what have you dreamed recently about this war's outcome?"

"Last night the gods themselves showed me a vision — I fasted and prayed for them to give me information. I saw Jove's bird, the Roman eagle, fly from the damp south to this part of the west, where it vanished in the sunbeams, which portends — unless my sins interfere with my divination — success to the Roman army."

"Dream such dreams often, and may they always be true," Caius Lucius replied.

Seeing Imogen (Fidele) and the corpse, he said, "Wait! What trunk is here without his top? The ruin shows that once this was a worthy building. What! A page! Either dead, or sleeping on him? But the page must be dead because it is not natural for him to make his bed by the deceased or to sleep on a corpse."

Referring to Imogen (Fidele), he ordered, "Let's see the boy's face."

The Captain said, "He's alive, my lord."

"He'll tell us about this body," Caius Lucius said.

He then said to Imogen (Fidele), "Young one, tell us about your fortunes, for it seems they must be told. Who is this whom you are making your bloody pillow? Or tell us who was he who has altered that good picture otherwise than noble nature did. What's your interest in this sad wreck? How came this to be? Who is he? Who are you?"

"I am nothing," Imogen (Fidele) said. "Or if I am not nothing, it would be better if I were nothing. This was my master. He is a very good and valiant Briton who was slain here by mountaineers. Alas! There are no more such masters as he. I may wander from the east to the west, cry out for employment, try many masters, all good, and serve them truly and loyally, but never find another such master."

"I pity you, good youth!" Caius Lucius said. "You move me no less with your grieving than your master moves me with his bleeding. Tell me his name, good friend."

"He was named Richard du Champ," Imogen (Fidele) replied.

She thought, *If I lie but do no harm by lying, then if the gods hear my lie, I hope they'll pardon it.*

Seeing Caius Lucius looking expectantly at her, she asked, "Did you say something, sir?"

"What is your name?"

"Fidele, sir."

"You have proven that you are faithful, as your name says that you are. Your name fits your faith well, and your faith fits your name well. Will you take a chance and serve me? Will you enter my employ? I will not say you shall have as good a master as you did, but you can be sure that you will be no less beloved than you were. The Roman Emperor's letters, sent by a consul to me, should not sooner than your own worth recommend you to me. Come, go with me and be in my employ."

"I'll follow you, sir," Imogen (Fidele) said. "But first, if it please the gods, I'll hide my dead master from the flies, as deep as these poor pickaxes — my fingers — can dig; and when with wild tree leaves and weeds I have strewn his grave, and on it said a hundred prayers that I know, twice, I'll weep and sigh. Then, leaving his service, I will follow you, if it pleases you to employ me."

"Yes, it does please me, good youth! And I will be more of a father to you than a master," Caius Lucius said.

He then ordered, "My friends, the boy has taught us manly duties. Let us find the prettiest daisied plot we can, and make a grave with our pikes and partisans for the boy's master. Come, carry the body in your arms."

Pikes and partisans are long-handled weapons.

He then said to Imogen (Fidele), "Boy, your late master is recommended by you to us, and he shall be interred as well as soldiers can inter him. Be cheerful; wipe your eyes. Some falls are the means for happier things to arise. Good can come from evil."

In a room in Cymbeline's palace stood King Cymbeline, some lords, Pisanio, and some attendants. The Queen was not present because she was very ill.

Cymbeline ordered an attendant, "Go again to the Queen, and bring me word how she is."

The attendant exited.

Cymbeline said, "The Queen has a fever because of the absence of her son. The fever is a result of madness, and her life's in danger. Heavens, how deeply all at once you wound me with many cares! Imogen, who is a great part of my comfort and happiness, is gone. My Queen is desperately ill in bed. And at a time when I face fearful wars and her son is much needed, he is gone. These blows take from me all hope of happiness."

He then said to Pisanio, "But as for you, fellow, who necessarily must know of Imogen's departure although you pretend that you are ignorant of it, we'll force you to give us information by using sharp, painful torture."

"Sir, my life is yours," Pisanio replied. "I humbly set it before you to do with as you will, but as for my mistress, I know nothing about where she is, why she is gone, or when she intends to return to the court. I beg your Highness to regard me as your loyal servant."

The first lord said, "My good liege, the day that Imogen was missed, Pisanio was here. I dare to vouch that he is loyal and shall perform all points of his service to you loyally. As for Cloten, we lack no diligence in seeking for him, and he will, no doubt, be found."

"These times are troubled," Cymbeline said.

He said to Pisanio, "We'll allow you to be free for a while, but our suspicions still hang over you."

"So please your majesty," the first lord said, "the Roman legions, all drawn from France, have landed on your coast, with a supply of Roman gentlemen sent by the Roman Senate."

"Now I wish I had the counsel of my son and my Queen!" Cymbeline said. "I am bewildered by so many important matters."

"My good liege," the first lord said, "your prepared and ready military forces can confront all the opposing forces that you have heard about. If more opposing forces come, you're ready for them. All that is needed now is to put those military forces in motion — they already long to be employed."

"I thank you," Cymbeline said. "Let's withdraw and meet the time as it seeks us. We don't fear what comes from Italy to annoy us, but we grieve because of the other events that have happened here. Let's go."

Everyone except Pisanio exited.

Pisanio said to himself, "I have received no letter from my master, Posthumus, since I wrote him that Imogen was slain — it is strange. Nor have I heard from Imogen, who promised to often send me news. Neither do I know what has happened to Cloten. I remain perplexed and in doubt about everything. The Heavens still must do their work and bring all to a good conclusion.

"When I am false, I am honest; I am not true because I can't be true if I want to be true. I lie so that I can serve Posthumus and Imogen honestly and truly and faithfully. My service in this present war shall show that I love my country, bringing me recognition even from the King, or I'll fall in the war.

"Let all other doubts be cleared by time. Fortune brings in some boats that are not steered.

"I can't resolve all doubts by myself; fortunately, in time some boats, even though they lack a pilot, make it safely into the harbor."

In Wales, in front of their cave, Belarius (Morgan), Guiderius (Polydore), and Arviragus (Cadwal) talked together.

Guiderius (Polydore) said, "The noise of soldiers preparing for war is all around us."

"Let's get away from it," Belarius (Morgan) said.

"What pleasure, sir, shall we find in life, if we lock life up and keep it away from action and adventure?" Arviragus (Cadwal) asked.

Guiderius (Polydore) added, "And what are we are hoping for by hiding ourselves? If we hide, the Romans will find us and either slay us because we are Britons, or they will believe that we are barbarous and unnatural rebels whom they can use for a while and then slay afterward."

"Sons," Belarius (Morgan) said, "we'll go higher in the mountains; there we will safely hide ourselves. We can't go and join the King's party. Because of Cloten's death — since we are not known to the King, and are not mustered among his forces — we may be forced to say where we have lived, and so they may extort from us the information that we have killed Cloten, and his death will result in our torture and death."

"Sir, this fear in you at such a time does not become you, nor does it make us happy," Guiderius (Polydore) said.

"It is not likely that when the British forces hear the Roman horses neigh, see the fires in the Romans' camps, and have their eyes and their ears so crammed with important matters as they are now, that they will waste their time on us and want to know from whence we have come," Arviragus (Cadwal) said.

"I am known by many people in the army," Belarius (Morgan) said. "The last time I saw Cloten he was then young, but the many years that have passed did not erase him from my memory, as you have seen. And, besides, the King has not deserved my service or your respect. You have found in sharing my exile a lack of education and proper training as well as the certainty of this hard life. You cannot hope to have the courtly style that your birth as my sons in the court promised you; instead, you will always be the tanned ones of the hot summer and the shrinking, shivering slaves of winter."

"It would be better not to exist than to be that," Guiderius (Polydore) said. "Please, sir, my brother and I are not known to the army. You, yourself, will not be questioned because you have been away so long that they no longer think about you. Also, your white hair and beard have so grown that they will not recognize you."

"By this Sun that shines," Arviragus (Cadwal) said, "I'll go and join the British soldiers. How shameful it is that I have never seen a man die! I have scarcely ever looked at blood, except that of coward hares, lecherous goats, and venison! I have never bestrode a horse, except one that had a rider like myself, who never wore a roweled spur or iron on his heel! I am ashamed to look upon the holy Sun, to have the benefit of the Sun's blest beams, because I have remained for so long a poor man with no reputation."

"By the Heavens, I'll go," Guiderius (Polydore) said. "If you will bless me, sir, and give me permission to leave, things will be better for me, but if you will not bless me, then let the danger that arises from being unblessed by you fall on me by the hands of the Romans!"

"Amen!" Arviragus (Cadwal) said.

"Since you set so slight a value on your lives, there is no reason why I should take more care of my cracked — wrinkled — life," Belarius (Morgan) said. "I am ready to go with you, boys! If you chance to die in your country's wars, a grave will be my bed, too, lads, and there I'll lie. Lead on! Lead on!"

He thought, *The time seems long; their blood thinks scorn, until it flies out and shows them to be Princes born. The time has come. They will scorn themselves until they are able to prove that they are true Princes.*

CHAPTER 5

— 5.1 —

Posthumus stood in the Roman camp in Britain, looking at a bloody cloth he held in his hand. Pisanio had sent him the bloody cloth as evidence that he had killed Imogen. Of course, Pisanio had not killed Imogen, despite Posthumus' order to kill her.

Posthumus said, "Yes, bloody cloth, I'll keep you, for I wished you should be colored red like this. Anyone who is married, if each of you should take this course of revenge that I have taken, then many of you will murder wives much better than yourselves simply because your wives strayed a little from the path of virtue!

"Oh, Pisanio! Every good servant obeys not all commands. There is no obligation to obey any commands except the just ones.

"Gods! If you had taken vengeance on my faults, I never would have lived to commit this wrong. You should have saved the noble Imogen so she could repent, and you should have struck me, a wretch more worth your vengeance. But, unfortunately, you snatch some from the world of the living because they committed little faults; still, that's showing them love because you don't allow them to sin any more. You also permit some to reinforce old sins with new sins, each later sin worse, and so eventually make the sinners dread sin, to the sinners' spiritual benefit.

"But Imogen is your own now. Gods, do your best wills, and make me blest to obey your wills! I have been brought here among the Italian gentry, so I can fight against my lady's — Imogen's — Kingdom.

"It is enough, Britain, that I have killed your mistress. Peace! I'll give no wound to you. Therefore, good Heavens, hear patiently what I intend to do. I'll take off these Italian clothes and put on the clothing of a British peasant, and dressed like that I'll fight against the army I came here with. In that way, I'll die for you, Imogen, for whom my life is every breath a death. Thus, unknown, neither pitied nor hated, I will dedicate myself to face danger. Let me make men know that more valor and courage are in me than my peasant clothing shows.

"Gods, put the strength of the Leonati family in me! To shame the usual practice of the world, I will begin the fashion of showing less on the outside and more on the inside. Internal valor and courage are better than fashionable clothing."

Leonati is the plural of *Leonatus*.

The battle began, with the forces of Caius Lucius and Iachimo making up the Roman army, which fought the British. Fighting on the side of the British was Posthumus Leonatus, who was dressed in the clothing of a peasant. At one point in the battle, Posthumus fought and defeated Iachimo, who did not recognize him. Posthumus did not kill Iachimo, but simply disarmed him and left him alive.

Iachimo said to himself, "The heaviness and guilt within my bosom are taking away my manhood. I have told lies about a lady, Imogen, the Princess of Britain, and the air of Britain gets revenge by making me feeble and weak. Otherwise, this churl, this natural-born peasant, this drudge of nature, would never have defeated me — fighting is my profession! Knighthoods and honors, borne as I wear mine, are titles only of scorn. Britain, if your gentry is that much better than this lout as he is better than our Italian lords, the odds are that we Italians are scarcely men and you Britons are gods."

The battle continued, and the Romans began to win. The British, routed, fled. King Cymbeline was captured, but Belarius (Morgan), Guiderius (Polydore), and Arviragus (Cadwal) arrived and began to fight to free him.

Belarius (Morgan) shouted to the retreating British soldiers, "Stand your ground! Stand your ground! We have the advantage of the ground. The lane is guarded. Nothing can rout us except our villainous fears!"

Guiderius (Polydore) and Arviragus (Cadwal) shouted, "Stand, stand, and fight!"

Posthumus Leonatus showed up and joined Belarius (Morgan), Guiderius (Polydore), and Arviragus (Cadwal). Together, they rescued King Cymbeline and took him to safety.

In another part of the battlefield, Caius Lucius stood with Iachimo and Imogen (Fidele).

Caius Lucius said to Imogen (Fidele), "Get away, boy, from the troops, and save yourself. In the confusion, friends are killing friends, and the disorder is such that it is as if soldiers were fighting while wearing blindfolds."

Iachimo said, "The British are benefitting from fresh reinforcements."

Caius Lucius said, "It is a day whose fortunes have turned strangely. We were winning, but now we are losing. It is time either to regroup or to flee."

After the battle, Posthumus Leonatus, still wearing the clothing of a British peasant, met a British lord.

The lord asked him, "Have you come from the place where our soldiers have made a stand against the Romans?"

"I did. But you, it seems, come from the soldiers who were fleeing."

"I did," the lord replied.

"I don't blame you, sir, because all was lost, except that the Heavens fought on our side. King Cymbeline himself was in trouble, the wings of his army were destroyed, the rest of his army was broken, and only the backs of British soldiers could be seen because all of them were fleeing through a straight lane.

"The enemy was full-hearted, with their tongues hanging out like wolves as they slaughtered British soldiers. The number of British soldiers available to be killed was more numerous than Roman weapons could handle. The Romans killed some British soldiers, mortally wounded some others, lightly wounded some others, and frightened some others so badly that they fell down simply out of fear. The narrow pass became dammed with men who died from the wounds they received while running away and with cowards who were not wounded but will live with shame until they die."

"Where was this lane?" the lord asked.

"Nearby the battlefield. It was sunken, and walled with turf. This gave an advantage to an old, experienced soldier, an honorable one, I promise you, who deserves to be honored by his country for as many years as it took him to grow his long beard and have it turn white.

"He and two striplings faced the Romans. The striplings were lads more likely to play boyish games than to commit such slaughter, and they had delicate faces that were fit to wear masks such as women wear to protect their faces from the Sun — actually, the boys' faces were even fairer than those of ladies who wear such masks to protect themselves from the Sun or to protect themselves from being stared at.

"The old man and the two boys made secure the narrow path. The old man shouted to those who fled, 'British deer die while fleeing, not our men. May souls who flee and retreat now quickly make their way to the darkness of Hell!

Stand your ground, or my sons and I will be Romans and will give you that beastly death that you shun like cowards. If you want to save your lives, all you need to do is turn around and frown at the Roman soldiers. Stand your ground! Stand your ground!'

"These three, who had the confidence of three thousand soldiers, and who in action were worth as many — for three soldiers are the army when all the rest of the soldiers do nothing — with this word 'Stand! Stand!' were able to put color into pale faces. They were given an advantage by the narrowness of the place, and they were all the more persuasive because of their own nobleness, which could have turned a woman using a distaff into a soldier using a lance. Some fleeing soldiers they shamed but they also renewed their spirit, and some, who had fled simply because others were fleeing — a sin in war, and damned in the first beginners! — began to look like the old man and his two sons, and to turn toward the Roman soldiers, and to grin like lions at the pikes of the hunters.

"Then the chasers began to stop, and then to retreat, and soon there was a rout, with thick confusion; and then the Roman soldiers fled like chickens back up the same path down which they had swooped like eagles. The same path they had strode like victors they now strode like slaves.

"And now our British cowards, like fragments of food during hard voyages, became the means of survival in an emergency. The Roman soldiers were fleeing, exposing their backs to the British, and the back door was open that led to their unguarded hearts — as they fled, their exposed and unguarded backs became a target to strike to reach their hearts! Heavens, how the former cowards wounded the fleeing Romans!

"Some cowards who had pretended to be dead or dying, and some of these cowards' friends whom the fierceness of the Romans had overcome, now fought back. Previously, one Roman soldier had chased ten British soldiers, but now each British soldier slaughtered twenty Roman soldiers. Those who had previously preferred to flee rather than resist, although fleeing meant dying, now became war machines on the battlefield."

The lord said, "This was a strange joining together: a narrow lane, an old man, and two boys."

"No, do not wonder at it," Posthumus replied. "You are made to wonder at the things you hear rather than to yourself do anything that would cause wonder in others. You seem like a person who would mock heroism rather than yourself do anything heroic.

"Will you satirically rhyme upon this event, and then recite your poem so you can mock it? Here are two lines you can use:

"*Two boys, an old man twice a boy, a lane,*

"*Preserved the Britons, and were the Romans' bane.*"

In the satiric lines, the old man was "twice a boy" because of senility; he was in his second childhood.

"Don't be angry, sir," the lord said.

Posthumus replied, "*Why would I be angry? For what end?*

"*Of anyone who does not dare to face his foe, I'll be the friend,*

"*For if he'll do as he is made to do,*

"*I know he'll quickly flee from my friendship, too.*

"You have forced me to rhyme and make satiric verses."

"Farewell," the lord said. "You're angry."

"Are you still fleeing?" Posthumus asked.

The lord exited.

"This is a lord!" Posthumus exclaimed. "Oh, noble misery, to be in the battlefield, and yet to have to ask me, 'What is the news?'

"Today how many British soldiers would have given their honors away in order to have saved their carcasses! They took to their heels to save their lives, and yet they died, nevertheless! I, protectively charmed in my own woe, could not find Death where I heard Death groan, nor could I feel Death where he struck. Being that Death is an ugly monster, it is strange that he hides himself in fresh cups, soft beds, and sweet words, and it is strange that he has more ministers than we who draw his knives in the war.

"Well, I will find Death. For the time being he favors the British and keeps them alive."

Posthumus took off his British-peasant clothing and said, "I am no longer a Briton. I have resumed again the part that I had when I came to Britain from Italy: I am a Roman soldier.

"I will fight no more, but I will surrender to the lowest peasant who shall touch my shoulder in the act of arrest. Great is the slaughter the Romans have made here; great is the retribution that the British must take.

"As for me, the only ransom I will offer will be death. I have come here to die, whether as a Roman or as a Briton. I will not keep breathing here or elsewhere; I will find some way to stop breathing because of what I did to Imogen."

Two British Captains and some British soldiers came onto the scene.

The first Captain said, "Great Jupiter be praised! The Roman General Caius Lucius has been captured. It is thought that the old man and his sons were angels."

The second Captain replied, "There was a fourth man, wearing peasants' clothing, who made the attack with them."

"So it is reported, but none of them can be found," the first Captain said.

Seeing Posthumus, now dressed like a Roman soldier, the first Captain said, "Stop! Who's there?"

Posthumus replied, "A Roman, who would not now be drooping here, if reinforcements had come to him."

The second Captain ordered, "Arrest him; he is a dog! No dog — or even a leg of a dog — shall return to Rome to tell about the crows that have pecked Roman corpses here. He brags about his service as if he were a man of reputation. Take him to King Cymbeline."

King Cymbeline, Belarius (Morgan), Guiderius (Polydore), Arviragus (Cadwal), and Pisanio arrived, along with some British soldiers and attendants, and some Roman prisoners. The Captains presented Posthumus Leonatus to King Cymbeline, who did not recognize him. Posthumus was then handed over to a jailer.

In an open area near the British camp stood Posthumus Leonatus and two jailors. Posthumus felt guilty because he believed that he had caused Imogen to die.

The first jailer bound Posthumus' hands and feet and said, "Now you are like an animal whose leg has been bound so that it can graze in a pasture but not wander off and be stolen. Since you are wearing fetters in this field, go ahead and graze if you find pasture."

The second jailer said, "Yes, if you find edible pasture and are hungry enough to eat it."

The jailers left, and Posthumus, now alone, said to himself, "Bondage, you are very welcome to me because, I think, you are a way for me to reach liberty. I am better off than a man who is sick with the gout since he will continue for a long time to groan in pain than be quickly cured by the sure physician, Death, who is the key that will open these fetters. My conscience, you are fettered by guilt. You are fettered more securely than my legs and wrists are. You good gods, give me penitence so that I can release the fetter that binds my mind, and then, after I am penitent, I can die and be free of guilt forever.

"Is it enough that I am sorry for causing Imogen to die? By feeling sorry, children appease their Earthly fathers; the gods are more full of mercy than are Earthly fathers.

"Must I repent? I cannot repent better than in fetters, which I desire and so they are not forced on me.

"If the main part of making amends for my sin is to give up my freedom, I can give up no more than my all — my life.

"Gods, I know that you are more merciful than are vile men, who from their broken debtors take a third of what they have, and then a sixth, and then a tenth, letting them 'thrive' again on their remaining means so that the creditor can take more at a later date.

"In order for me to pay for Imogen's dear life, take mine, and although my life is not as dear as her life, yet it is a life. You created and coined it. When money passes from one man to another, they do not weigh every coin to make sure that it has the correct weight. Even though some coins may be light of weight, the men treat the coins as being worth the figure stamped on them. I am stamped in your image, and so, great powers, if you will take me although I am light of weight through having sinned, then take this life of mine, and let it pay my debt in full.

"Oh, Imogen! I'll speak to you in silence."

He lay on the ground and slept.

Solemn music could be heard, and Posthumus' dead relatives and other beings began to appear. First some musicians appeared. Then Posthumus' father, Sicilius Leonatus, appeared; he was an old man who was dressed like a warrior. Sicilius held the hand of a mature woman who was his wife and Posthumus' mother. Next appeared Posthumus' two brothers; the mortal wounds that they had received in battle could be seen. All of these ghosts surrounded Posthumus as he slept.

Sicilius Leonatus said, "Bestow your spite no more, Jupiter, you thunder-master, on mortal flies such as Posthumus. Instead, bestow your spite on the gods. Quarrel with Mars, the god of war, and chide Juno, your wife, who hates your adulteries and criticizes them and gets revenge on them. Has my poor boy Posthumus, whose face I never saw in the world of the living, done anything but good? I died while he was still in the womb waiting for the time he would obey nature's law and be born. Men say that you act as the father to orphans, and therefore you are Posthumus' non-biological father. You should have acted like his father and shielded him from the grief of this tormenting Earthy life."

Posthumus' mother said, "The goddess of childbirth, Lucina, did not give me her aid. Instead, she took my life when I was supposed to give birth. From my body Posthumus was ripped. He came crying into the midst of his enemies; he was a thing of pity!"

Sicilius, Posthumus' father, said, "Great nature, like his ancestry, molded Posthumus so well that he deserved the praise of the world — he was the heir of great Sicilius."

The first brother said, "When Posthumus became a mature man, where was the man in Britain who was his equal or who could be as promising a man in the eyes of Imogen, who best can appraise Posthumus' worth?"

Posthumus' mother said, "Once he married Imogen, why, Jupiter, did you mock him by allowing him to be thrown from the estate of the Leonati family and exiled from his dearest one, sweet Imogen?"

Sicilius, Posthumus' father, said, "Why, Jupiter, did you allow Iachimo, that slight thing of Italy, to taint Posthumus' nobler heart and brain with needless jealousy, and to become the sucker and scorn of Iachimo's villainy?"

The second brother said, "We — Posthumus' parents and his two brothers, who fought and died bravely for our country — came from stiller seats in the happy fields of Elysium, where the blest spirits of the dead reside. We want to maintain with honor our loyalty and the right that King Tenantius, King Cymbeline's father, gave us. Tenantius gave our family the name Leonatus; for our family honor to be upheld, Posthumus must be treated with the respect he deserves."

The first brother said, "We performed daring deeds in battle for King Tenantius, and Posthumus has performed daring deeds in battle for King Cymbeline. Why, then, Jupiter, you King of gods, have you postponed giving Posthumus the honors he deserves, and instead are giving him sorrows?"

Sicilius, Posthumus' father, said, "Jupiter, open the clear crystal window of your Heavenly palace, and look out. No longer exercise upon a valiant family your harsh and potent injuries. No longer use your power to treat Posthumus so harshly."

Posthumus' mother said, "Since, Jupiter, our son is good, take away his miseries."

Sicilius, Posthumus' father, said, "Peep through your marble mansion and help, or we poor ghosts will cry to the shining assembly of the rest of the gods against your deity."

The word "marble" referred to a kind of pattern of light and color seen in the sky — imagine the Sun shining through parts of a cloudy sky so that it is "aglow with lacing streaks," in the words of Shakespearean scholar Horace Howard Furniss, editor of *Othello* and other plays by Shakespeare.

Posthumus' two brothers cried, "Help, Jupiter; or we will appeal to other gods, and flee from your justice."

Jupiter heard the Leonati family's prayers. Thunder sounded and lightning struck, and Jupiter, sitting on an eagle, flew down to Earth as he threw an additional thunderbolt. The ghosts of the Leonati family fell to their knees before him.

Jupiter said to them, "You petty spirits of the low region, the abode of the dead, offend me no more with your complaints. Be silent! How dare you ghosts accuse me, the thunderer, whose thunderbolt, as you know, is planted in the sky and batters all rebelling coasts?

"You poor shadows of Elysium, leave this place, and rest upon your never-withering banks of flowers. Don't distress yourselves with mortal events. They are no concerns of yours; you know that they are my concerns.

"Those whom I love best I thwart; the more delayed I make my gift, the more it delights when it arrives. Be patient; our godhead will uplift your low-laid son. His comforts will thrive, and his trials are almost over.

"Our majestic star — Jupiter, the planet of justice — reigned at Posthumus' birth, and in our temple he was married.

"Rise, you ghosts, and fade back to Elysium.

"Posthumus shall be the lord and husband of Lady Imogen, and his afflictions will make him much happier than if he had never endured them."

Jupiter gave Sicilius a tablet and said, "Lay this tablet upon his breast."

The outside of the tablet was richly decorated; inside the tablet words were written.

Jupiter continued, "On this tablet I have written Posthumus' full future. Once you have laid this tablet on his chest, all of you spirits leave. Complain no more, lest you make me angry.

"Climb, eagle, to my crystalline palace."

Jupiter flew away on the eagle.

Sicilius Leonatus said, "Jupiter came in thunder; his celestial breath was sulfurous to smell. The holy eagle swooped as if to clutch us with its talons. Where Jupiter ascends is sweeter than our blest fields in Elysium. Jupiter's royal bird, the eagle, trims the feathers of its immortal wings and uses its claws to scratch its beak — this shows that Jupiter is pleased."

All the spirits of the Leonati family prayed, "Thanks, Jupiter!"

Sicilius Leonati said, "The marble pavement of Heaven closes, Jupiter has entered his radiant home. Let's leave! And, in order to be blest, let us carefully perform Jupiter's great command."

He placed the tablet on Posthumus' chest, and then the spirits vanished.

Posthumus Leonatus woke up and said, "Sleep, you have been a grandfather and have begotten a father to me, and you have created for me a mother and two brothers. But, this is a bitter joke — they went away from here as soon as they were born, and so I am awake.

"Poor wretches who depend on the favor of great ones for their life dream as I have just done, and they wake up and find nothing. But, alas, I am wrong. Many people do not dream in order to find blessings, and they do not deserve to find blessings, and yet they receive blessings. I am in that situation. I want to die, and yet I have this golden event — this golden dream — and I do not know why."

He felt the tablet on his chest and said, "What fairies haunt this ground? A tablet? It's a rare and exceptional one! Don't be, as is common in our fashion-obsessed world, a garment that is nobler than what it covers. Let the words written within your pages be as noble as what covers them, unlike our courtiers."

He read the words of the tablet out loud:

"*When a lion's whelp shall, to himself unknown, without seeking find, and be embraced by a piece of tender air; and when from a stately cedar shall be lopped branches, which, being dead many years, shall afterward revive, be joined to the old stock and freshly grow, then Posthumus shall end his miseries, and Britain shall be fortunate and flourish in peace and plenty.*"

Posthumus did not understand the meaning of the words, but a soothsayer would later explain them.

He said to himself, "This is still a dream that I am having, or else it is such nonsense as madmen speak and don't understand.

"Here are more possibilities: Either it is both of these or it is nothing; that is, either it is the speaking of a madman in a dream, or it is nothing."

Madmen and "madmen" can speak falsely or truthfully, although what they say sounds like nonsense. The same is true of prophets and "prophets."

He continued, "But the words on the tablet are a kind of speaking: The words on the tablet are the words of a prophecy, whether false or true. Therefore, either it is senseless speaking, or it is a speaking such as reason cannot untie — such speaking may be full of sense although I am not able to understand it.

"Whatever the words on this tablet mean, the action of my life is like them — difficult to understand, or perhaps senseless — and I'll keep the tablet, if only because of the words' resemblance to my life."

The first jailer returned and said to Posthumus, "Come, sir, are you ready for death?"

"I am more than ready," Posthumus replied. "If I were a piece of meat, I would be over-roasted; that is, I would have been ready for the dining table long ago."

The first jailer replied, "Roasted meat is hung up so that its aging improves the flavor, sir. If you are ready to be hung, you are well cooked."

"So, if I prove to be a good repast to the spectators, then the dish pays the shot," Posthumus said.

The dish is food, and the shot is a reckoning — the bill. For some spectators, a hanging is a good repast — good entertainment. And before and after the entertainment, chances are excellent that spectators would go to a tavern and buy a drink, thereby giving the innkeeper a very profitable day. Posthumus' hanging would draw in a big audience and help the innkeeper pay his bills.

The first jailor said, "That is a heavy reckoning for you, sir. But your comfort is that you shall be called to no more payments; you will fear no more tavern bills, which are often the sadness of parting, although the bills also procure mirth. You come in faint for lack of food, and then you depart reeling with too much drink. You are sorry that you have paid too much, and you are sorry that you are paid too much — drinking too much alcohol pays you back with a hangover. Your wallet and your brain are both empty. Your brain is all the heavier in the morning for being too light the previous night. Your wallet is too light because the drawing of beers resulted in drawing out of your wallet the money that had made it heavy. Death pays all bills, so by dying you won't have to worry about these contradictions.

"Oh, the charity of a penny rope that is used in a hanging! It gives a reckoning of thousands of bills in a trice — a single pull on the gallows and in an instant. You will have no true debit or credit but death. You will be released for all liability for what is past, what is present, and what is to come. Your neck, sir, is pen, book, and counting pieces, so the exoneration of all your debts and the deliverance from all your troubles follow."

"I am merrier to die than you are to live," Posthumus said.

"Indeed, sir, he who sleeps does not feel the toothache, but I think a man who was going to sleep your permanent sleep would change places with the hangman who intended to help him to bed — the grave — because you see, sir, you don't know which way you shall go when you die."

"Yes, indeed, I do, fellow."

"Your Death has eyes in his head then," the first jailer said. "I have not seen the personification of Death so pictured — usually, he is depicted as a skeleton, including an empty skull. You must either be instructed by some who take upon them to know about Death, or you take upon yourself that which I am sure you do not know, or you risk the Final Judgment at your own peril, and I think you'll never return to tell anyone in the living world how you shall speed in your journey's end."

"I tell you, fellow, there are none who lack eyes to direct them the way I am going, but such people close their eyes and will not use them."

Posthumus was ready to die. He had repented his sin, and he was ready to atone for his sin by dying. Other men and women, if they wanted, could repent their sins and atone for them and so be ready to die.

The first jailer said, "What an infinite act of mockery is this, that a man should have the best use of his eyes to see the way of blindness! I am sure hanging's a good way of closing one's eyes."

A messenger arrived and said to the first jailer, "Knock off his manacles; bring your prisoner to the King."

"You bring good news," Posthumus said. "I am called to be made free."

By "be made free," Posthumus meant "be hanged."

"I'll be hanged then," the first jailer said.

"You shall be then freer than a jailer," Posthumus said. "There are no fetters for the dead."

Posthumus and the messenger exited.

Alone, the first jailer said to himself, "Unless a man would marry a gallows and beget young gibbets, I never saw a man so eager to climb onto a gallows. Yet, on my conscience, there are worse knaves than this Roman who desire to live. This man is a Roman, and Romans are stoic and are supposed to not care about death, but there are some Romans, too, who die against their wills. So should I, if I were a Roman. I wish that we were all of one mind, and that one mind good. If that should happen, then there would be a desolation of jailers and gallows! I would lose my job, so what I am saying is against my present profit, but my wish has a preferment in it — I prefer a better world with better people and a better job for me."

— 5.5 —

In front of King Cymbeline's tent stood Cymbeline, Belarius (Morgan), Guiderius (Polydore), and Arviragus (Cadwal). Although Cymbeline did not know it, Polydore was his older son, Guiderius, and Cadwal was his younger son, Arviragus. Morgan was Belarius, a general whom Cymbeline had exiled years ago. To get revenge, Belarius (Morgan) had kidnapped Cymbeline's two sons. Also present were Pisanio and some lords, military officers, and attendants.

King Cymbeline said to Belarius (Morgan), Guiderius (Polydore), and Arviragus (Cadwal), "Stand by my side, you whom the gods have made preservers of my throne. My heart is sorrowful because the peasant soldier who so splendidly fought, whose rags shamed the gilded armor of other soldiers, who with his naked breast stepped before shields of proven strength, cannot be found. Whoever can find him shall be happy, if our recognition and respect can make him happy."

"I never saw such noble fury in so poor a thing," Belarius (Morgan) said. "I never saw such precious deeds done by one whose looks promised nothing except beggary and poverty."

"Is there no news of him?" Cymbeline asked.

Pisanio replied, "He has been searched for among the dead and the living, but there is no trace of him."

"To my grief, I am the heir of his reward," Cymbeline said. "I still have what I would have given to him."

He said to Belarius (Morgan), Guiderius (Polydore), and Arviragus (Cadwal), "But I will add what I would have given to him to you, who are metaphorically the liver, heart, and brain — the vital organs — of Britain, and I grant that she lives because of you three. It is now time for me to ask from where you come. Tell me."

"Sir, we were born in Cambria," Belarius (Morgan) said.

Cambria is the Latin name for Wales.

He continued, "We are gentlemen. For us to further boast would be neither virtuous nor modest, unless I add that we are honest and of good character."

"Bow your knees," King Cymbeline commanded.

115

They knelt, and King Cymbeline knighted them and said, "Arise, my knights of the battlefield. I now make you companions to our person and will give you dignities that are becoming to your new rank and status."

Doctor Cornelius and some ladies arrived.

Seeing them, Cymbeline said, "From their faces, I can see that they have come about serious business."

He said to them, "Why do you welcome our victory so sadly? You look like Romans, not like you are part of the court of Britain."

Doctor Cornelius said, "Hail, great King! Although it will sour your happiness, I must report to you that the Queen is dead."

"Who worse than a physician could this report come from?" Cymbeline replied. "But I realize that although life may be prolonged by medicine, yet death will seize the doctor, too. How did she die?"

"With horror, madly dying, like her life, which, being cruel to the world, ended most cruelly to herself," Doctor Cornelius said. "I will report what she confessed, if you want me to. These women, her female attendants, can correct me, if I err; they have wet cheeks and were present when the Queen died."

"Please, tell me how she died," Cymbeline requested.

Doctor Cornelius replied, "First, she confessed that she never loved you, that she loved only the great status she got by being married to you. She did not marry you for yourself. She married your royalty; she was wife to your place in society; she hated you."

"She alone knew this," Cymbeline said. "I did not know it. And, except that she spoke it as she was dying, I would not believe her lips as she said these things. Proceed."

"Your daughter, whom she pretended to love with such integrity, she confessed was actually like a scorpion to her sight. The Queen would have taken away your daughter's life by poisoning her except that your daughter's flight prevented it."

"The Queen was a most delicate fiend!" Cymbeline said. "Who can read a woman and know what she is thinking? Is there more?"

"Yes, there is more, sir, and it is worse," Doctor Cornelius said. "She confessed that she had ready for you a deadly poison, which, once you had taken it, would by each minute feed on your life and kill you little by little. During the lingering time during which you would die, she intended by watching over you, weeping over you, waiting on you, and kissing you, to overcome you with her pretense of loving you, and in time, after she had shaped you in such a way to accomplish her purpose, to work her son into the inheritance of the crown. However, she failed in her plan because of her son's strange absence, and so she grew shameless and desperate. She made known, in despite of Heaven and men, her plots. She repented only that the evils she had planned were not effected, and so in despair she died."

"Did you hear all this, my Queen's female attendants?"

One of the Queen's female attendants replied, "We did, so please your highness."

"My eyes were not at fault, for she was beautiful," Cymbeline said. "My ears, which heard her flattery, and my heart, which thought that she was like her appearance, were also not at fault because it would have been reprehensible to mistrust and misbelieve her. Yet my daughter may very well say, and have the experience to prove it, that I was foolish to have trusted my Queen. May Heaven mend all!"

Caius Lucius, Iachimo, the soothsayer, and other Roman prisoners arrived under guard. Posthumus Leonatus followed them, as did Imogen, who was still wearing male clothing and still using the name Fidele.

King Cymbeline said, "You do not now come, Caius Lucius, for the tribute that the Britons have erased with their victory, though we Britons have lost many bold soldiers who died on the battlefield. The kinsmen of those dead soldiers have requested of me to appease the good souls of these slaughtered soldiers with the slaughter of you Romans who are now our captives. We as King have granted their request. So think now of the state of your soul and prepare your body to die."

"Consider, sir, the chance of war," Caius Lucius replied. "The day was yours by fate; if fate had favored us, we Romans would have won the battle. Had victory come to us, we would not, when soldiers' blood and the heat of battle were cool, have threatened our prisoners with the sword. But since the gods will have it thus — that nothing but our lives may be called ransom — let death come. This is something that a Roman with a Roman's heart can endure. Augustus lives to think about this."

Caius Lucius believed that Caesar Augustus would send more Roman soldiers to conquer Britain and avenge the death of his soldiers, including Caius himself, and he wanted Cymbeline to think about this.

He continued, "So much for my individual concerns. One thing only I will ask you for. My young page is a Briton born. Let him be ransomed. Never has a master ever had a page who was so kind, so duteous, so diligent, so considerate over his occasions to serve me. He is so true and loyal, so adept at his duties, and so nurse-like. Let his virtue join with my request, which I strongly believe that your highness cannot deny. He has done no Briton harm, although he has served a Roman. Save him, sir, even if you spare no one else's life."

"I have surely seen him before," Cymbeline said. "His face is familiar to me."

He said to Imogen (Fidele), "Boy, your looks have made me favor you, and you are now my own servant. I don't know why, exactly, I say to you, 'Live, boy.' You need not thank your master, Caius Lucius, for your life since it is your own appearance that makes me give you mercy. Live, and ask from me, Cymbeline, whatever boon you want that is suitable for me to give and for you to take. I'll give that boon to you; I will grant your wish even if you demand that a prisoner, the noblest taken today, be spared from death."

Cymbeline was hoping to be able to spare the life of Caius Lucius, who had been a friend before the war.

"I humbly thank your highness," Imogen (Fidele) said.

"I do not ask you to beg that my life be saved, good lad," Caius Lucius said, "and yet I know you will do that."

"No, no," Imogen (Fidele) replied. "I'm sorry, but there's other work at hand: I see a thing that is as bitter to me as death. Your life, good master, must shift for itself."

Imogen (Fidele) was looking at Iachimo, and the thing that she saw that was as bitter to her as death was the diamond ring — the ring that she had given Posthumus — that he was wearing on his finger.

"The boy disdains me," Caius Lucius said. "He leaves me and scorns me. Quickly die the joys of those who make them depend on the loyalty of girls and boys."

He looked at Imogen (Fidele) more closely and asked, "Why does he look so perplexed?"

"What do you want, boy?" Cymbeline asked. "I love you more and more. Think more and more about what's best for you to ask for. Do you know the man you are looking at? Speak. Do you want him to live? Is he your kin? Is he your friend?"

"He is a Roman," Imogen (Fidele) replied, "and so he is no more kin to me than I am to your highness."

This was true of Fidele, if Fidele actually existed, but Imogen was Cymbeline's daughter, and so she added, "But I, being born your vassal, am somewhat nearer to you than I am to him."

"Why are you looking at him in that way?" Cymbeline asked.

"I'll tell you, sir, in private, if you please to give me a hearing."

"I will, with all my heart, and I will give you my best attention. What's your name?"

"Fidele, sir."

"You are my good youth; you are my page," Cymbeline said. "I'll be your employer. Walk with me; speak freely."

Cymbeline and Imogen (Fidele) spoke privately, away from the others.

Belarius (Morgan) said to Guiderius (Polydore) and Arviragus (Cadwal), "Has this boy been revived from death?"

"One grain of sand does not resemble another grain of sand more closely than this boy resembles that sweet rosy lad who died and was named Fidele," Arviragus (Cadwal) said.

He then asked his brother, "What do you think?"

"The same boy that we saw dead is now alive," Guiderius (Polydore) replied.

"Quiet! Quiet!" Belarius (Morgan) said. "Let's wait and see. He does not see us. Let's wait. Creatures may be alike. If this boy were our Fidele, I am sure that he would have spoken to us."

"But we saw him dead," Guiderius (Polydore) replied.

"Be quiet; let's wait and see," Belarius (Morgan) said.

Recognizing Imogen, Pisanio said, "It is my female boss. Since she is living, let the time run on, whether the end result is good or bad."

Cymbeline and Imogen (Fidele) rejoined the others.

Cymbeline said to Imogen (Fidele), "Come and stand by our side. State your demand out loud."

He ordered Iachimo, "Sir, step forward. Answer this boy's questions, and do it freely, or by our greatness and the power that goes with it, which is our honor, bitter torture shall winnow the truth from falsehood."

Iachimo stepped forward, and Cymbeline said to Imogen (Fidele), "Go on, speak to him."

Imogen (Fidele) said loudly, "The boon I ask for is that this gentleman tells from whom he got this ring."

Posthumus Leonatus thought, *What is my ring to him?*

Cymbeline said to Iachimo, "Say how you came to have this diamond ring that is on your finger."

Iachimo replied, "If I say that, it will torture you, and you will torture me to take it back."

"What? Torture me?" Cymbeline said.

"I am glad to be forced to utter that which torments me to conceal," Iachimo said. "I got this ring by villainy. This was Posthumus Leonatus' ring, whom you banished, and — which may grieve you more, as it does me — who is a nobler sir than any man who has ever lived between sky and ground. Will you hear more, my lord?"

"I want to hear everything that is relevant to him," Cymbeline replied.

"That paragon, your daughter — for whom my heart drops blood, and my false spirits quail to remember — give me permission to stop awhile. I am faint."

"My daughter! What about her? Regain your strength. I had rather you should live out your full natural life than die before I hear more. Make an effort, man, and speak."

"Once upon a time ... unhappy was the clock that struck the hour! ... it was in Rome ... accursed be the mansion where it happened! ... it was at a feast ... oh, I wish that all our food had been poisoned, or at least those bits of food that I heaved up to my head! ... the good Posthumus ... what should I say? He was too good to be where evil men were, and he was the best of all the men who are among the rarest and best of good men ... sitting sadly, hearing us praise our loves — our loved ones — of Italy.

"We praised our loves of Italy for their beauty — beauty that we said outdid even the biggest and most swelled boast that the man who could best speak about beauty could make.

"We praised our loves of Italy for their bodily features, features that we said in comparison made Venus lame in her shrine or that we said made tall, straight-backed Minerva lame. Both goddesses have postures much better than those of mortals who live only briefly.

"We praised our loves of Italy for their disposition, saying that our women were a shop of all the qualities that man loves woman for, besides that enticing hook that persuades men to take wives, that hook of women's beauty that strikes the eye —"

Impatient at Iachimo's flowery way of speaking, Cymbeline interrupted, "I stand on fire; I am impatient and angry. Get to the point."

"All too soon I shall," Iachimo replied, "unless you want to grieve quickly. This Posthumus, who was most like a noble lord in love and one who had a royal lover, took his opportunity, and, not dispraising those whom we praised — therein he was as calm as virtue — he began to paint in words his wife's picture, which once being made by his tongue, he added a description of her mind to it, and we realized that either our brags were crowing about kitchen girls, or his description proved that we were idiots who were incapable of speech."

"Get to the point," Cymbeline again ordered Iachimo.

"Your daughter's chastity — there it begins. Posthumus spoke about your daughter as if in comparison to her the virgin goddess Diana had lecherous wet dreams and your daughter alone were chaste. Hearing this, I, wretch that I am, objected to his praise, and I wagered with him pieces of gold against this diamond ring that he then wore upon his finger, which was honored by the wearing. I bet him that by wooing his wife I could attain his place in her bed and win this ring by persuading her to commit adultery.

"He, a true knight, was completely confident of her honor — I later found that he was truly justified in his confidence — and he bet this ring, and he would have bet it even if it had been a ruby from one of the wheels of Phoebus Apollo's Sun-chariot. Indeed, he could have safely bet his ring even if it had been worth what the entire Sun-chariot is worth.

"I hurried away to Britain to carry out the seduction I had planned. Well may you, sir, remember me visiting your court, where your chaste daughter taught me the wide difference between faithful love and adulterous love.

"My hope being thus quenched, although my lust was not quenched, my Italian brain began in your Britain, which is located in a northern climate that produces dullness, to operate most vilely and excellently for my profit. And, to be brief, the plot I thought up so prevailed that I returned with enough fake but plausible evidence to make the noble Leonatus mad — insane. I wounded his belief in his wife's reputation by doing such things as describing the wall tapestries and pictures in the bedchamber."

He pulled her bracelet out of his pocket and said, "I also showed him her bracelet — it was cunning how I got it from her. In addition, I described some hidden marks on her body. I provided so much spurious evidence that he could not but think that her bond of chastity was quite cracked and broken, and that I had won our bet.

"Whereupon — but I think that I see Posthumus now —"

Angry, Posthumus, who had been a short distance away but unnoticed by most of the people present, advanced toward Iachimo and said, "Yes, you do see me, you Italian fiend! Call me the most credulous fool, egregious murderer, thief, any name used to refer to all the villains in the past, the present, and the future! Oh, I wish that upright justice would give me a rope, or a knife, or poison to use to kill myself! King Cymbeline, send out for ingenious torturers: I make all the abhorred things of the Earth seem better by comparison because I am worse than they are. I am Posthumus, who killed your daughter — but like a villain, I lie — I caused a lesser villain than myself, a sacrilegious thief, to do the killing. She was the temple of Virtue, yes, and she herself was the personification of Virtue.

"Spit on, throw stones at, and cast mire upon me. Sic the dogs of the street on me! Let every villain be called Posthumus Leonatus, and let villainy be less than it was because it is compared to the villainy I have done!

"Oh, Imogen! My Queen, my life, my wife! Oh, Imogen, Imogen, Imogen!"

Imogen, still dressed as the young man Fidele, went to him and said, "Be calm, my lord; listen, listen —"

Posthumus interrupted her: "Shall we make a play out of what is happening here? You scornful page, there lies your part."

He hit her, and she fell down.

Pisanio, who had recognized Imogen because he was familiar with her disguise, said, "Oh, gentlemen, help! This is my employer and Posthumus' wife! Oh, my lord Posthumus! You never killed Imogen until now! Help, help! My honored lady!"

"Does the world still go around?" Cymbeline asked, shocked by such strange events.

"Why do I feel so faint?" Posthumus asked, staggering.

"Wake up, Imogen!" Pisanio cried.

"If this is truly Imogen," Cymbeline said, "then the gods mean to strike me dead by giving me more joy than I can take."

Pisanio said to Imogen, "How are you?"

Imogen, who thought that Pisanio had given her poison when he left her in Wales, said angrily to him, "Get out of my sight! You gave me poison! Dangerous fellow, leave here! Do not breathe where Princes are! Stay away from royalty!"

"That is the voice of Imogen!" Cymbeline cried.

"Lady," Pisanio said to Imogen, "may the gods throw stones of sulfur — thunderbolts — at me, if I did not think that box I gave you was a precious thing. I received it from the Queen."

"Still more revelations?" Cymbeline said.

"Its contents poisoned me," Imogen said.

Doctor Cornelius said, "Gods! I left out one thing that the Queen confessed, which will prove that Pisanio is honest and loyal. The Queen said, 'If Pisanio has given Imogen that confection that I gave him and told him that it was medicine, she is served as I would serve a rat. It is poison, and she will die.'"

"What's this all about, Cornelius?" Cymbeline asked.

"The Queen, sir, very often importuned me to mix poisons for her, always pretending that she wanted to gain knowledge by killing vile creatures, such as cats and dogs, of no esteem. I, fearing that she intended to do something more dangerous than that, mixed for her a certain substance, which, being taken, would stop the bodily functions that make people live, but after a short time all bodily parts would again do their due functions. The person swallowing some of the substance would 'die' — that is, appear to be dead — but only for a short time."

He asked Imogen, "Did you swallow some of that substance?"

"Most likely I did, because I was dead."

Belarius (Morgan) said to Guiderius (Polydore) and Arviragus (Cadwal), "My boys, we were wrong when we thought that Fidele was dead."

Guiderius (Polydore) said, "This is certainly Fidele."

Imogen said to Posthumus, "Why did you throw your wedded lady away from you? Imagine that you are standing upon a cliff, and throw me away from you now."

She embraced him tightly. They were together now until death.

Posthumus said to his wife, "Hang there like a fruit, my soul, until the tree dies!"

He embraced her tightly. They were together now until death.

Cymbeline said to Imogen, "Now, my flesh, my child! Are you making me a dullard in this act by not allowing me to speak any lines? Won't you speak to me?"

Imogen knelt before him and said, "I ask for your blessing, sir."

Belarius (Morgan) said to Guiderius (Polydore) and Arviragus (Cadwal), "Although you loved this youth, I don't blame you. You had a reason for it."

That reason, although Guiderius (Polydore) and Arviragus (Cadwal) did not know it, was that Imogen was their sister.

Cymbeline said, "May my tears that fall prove to be holy water falling on you! Imogen, your mother-in-law is dead."

"I am sorry, my lord," she replied.

"Oh, she was evil, and it is because of her that we meet here so strangely, but her son, Cloten, is gone — we don't know why or where."

Pisanio said, "My lord, now that I am no longer afraid, I'll speak the truth."

Pisanio had been afraid first, that Imogen was hurt, and second, that he would be unjustly punished for "poisoning" her.

He continued, "After my lady, Imogen, was discovered to be missing from court, Lord Cloten came to me with his sword drawn. He foamed at the mouth, and he swore that unless I revealed which way she had gone, he would instantly kill me. I happened to have a deceptive letter written by my master, Posthumus, in my pocket. I gave the letter to Cloten; it directed him to seek Imogen on the mountains near Milford Haven. Frenzied, and wearing Posthumus' clothing, which he forced me to bring to him, he hurried there with an unchaste purpose and with an oath to violate my lady's honor and rape her. What then became of him I don't know."

Guiderius (Polydore) said, "Let me end the story: I slew Cloten in Wales."

A commoner — or even a knight — killing a Prince was a serious offense, one that would be punished with death.

Cymbeline said, "The gods forbid! You have done deeds of note in battle for me, and killing the nobleman who wanted to rape my daughter is a notable good deed. I don't want such a good deed to pluck from my lips a hard sentence of death. Please, valiant youth, deny what you just said."

"I have spoken it, and I did it."

"The man you killed was a Prince," Cymbeline said.

"He was a very uncivil one," Guiderius (Polydore) said. "The wrongs he did me were not things that a Prince would do. He provoked me with language that would make me spurn the sea, if it could roar to me like Cloten did. I cut off his head, and I am very glad that he is dead and is not standing here telling you that he cut off my head."

"I am sorry for you," Cymbeline said. "You are condemned by your own tongue, and you must endure our law: You are sentenced to die."

Imogen said, "I thought that headless man was my husband."

"Bind the offender, and take him away from our presence," Cymbeline ordered.

"Wait, sir King," Belarius (Morgan) said. "This man you are arresting is better and higher in rank than the man he slew. In fact, he is as well descended as you are, and because of his battle scars he has earned more from you than a band of Clotens ever has."

He then said to the guards, "Let his arms alone; they were not born for bondage."

King Cymbeline was angry. In his view, to say that an impoverished man like Polydore, even though he was recently knighted, was descended as well as a King such as Cymbeline was an insult.

He said, "Why, old soldier, will you throw away the rewards that you have not yet received by making me angry and tasting of our wrath?"

Using the royal plural, he asked, "How can this man be descended as well as we are?"

Arviragus (Cadwal), who did not know that he was Cymbeline's son, said, "When Morgan made that claim, he claimed way too much."

Cymbeline said, "And you, Morgan, shall die for it."

Belarius (Morgan) said, referring to himself and his two "sons," "In the long run, all three of us will die. But I will prove that two of us are as well descended as I have said this man is."

He then said to Guiderius (Polydore) and Arviragus (Cadwal), "My 'sons,' I must unfold a speech that will be dangerous for me, although it will, fortunately, help you."

"Your danger is ours," Arviragus (Cadwal) said to Belarius (Morgan).

"And our good is his," Guiderius (Polydore) said to Arviragus (Cadwal).

"Let me do this, then, by your leave," Belarius (Morgan) said to Cymbeline. "You had, great King, a subject who was called Belarius."

"What about him? He is a banished traitor."

"He has become aged, and he is the man whom you see before you; he is indeed a banished man, but I do not know how he is a traitor."

Cymbeline ordered, "Take Belarius away. The whole world shall not save him."

"Not so hasty," Belarius replied. "First pay me for raising up your sons. If you want, confiscate all you pay me as soon as I have received my pay."

"The raising up of my sons!"

"I am too blunt and insolent," Belarius said. "I need to be more respectful."

He knelt and said, "Here's my knee. Before I arise, I will advance and promote my sons in life, and then you need not spare the old father. Mighty sir, these two young gentlemen, who call me father and think they are my sons, are not my sons. They are your sons. They are the issue of your loins, my liege, and they are blood of your begetting."

"What! My sons!"

"They are your sons as surely as you are your father's son. I, old Morgan, am that Belarius whom you once banished. I did no harm, but you thought I did, and it was your thoughts that caused me to be accused of and punished for treason. The only harm I did was to be unjustly punished for something I did not do.

"I have raised these gentle Princes — for such and so they are — for these past twenty years. I taught them those accomplishments that they have and that I was able to give them. My breeding was, sir, as your highness knows.

"Their nurse, Euriphile, whom I wedded because of the theft, kidnapped these children after I was banished. I persuaded her to do it. Having received the punishment before I did anything wrong, I did something that would deserve that punishment. Being beaten for having been loyal made me want to commit treason. The more that you would hurt because of the loss of your dear children, the more I wanted to steal them.

"But, gracious sir, here are your sons again; and I must lose two of the sweetest companions in the world. May the benediction and blessings of these covering Heavens fall on their heads like dew for they are worthy to inlay Heaven with stars. Once they die, they are worthy to become Heavenly constellations!"

Cymbeline said, "You weep, and speak. The service that you three have done is more remarkable than this story you tell me now. I believe the service you did for me in battle because I saw it, and therefore I ought now to believe your tears and your story. If these two young men are my sons, I don't know how I could wish for a pair of worthier sons."

Belarius said, "Be pleased awhile. This gentleman, whom I call Polydore, is really Guiderius, a most worthy Prince and your elder son."

"This gentleman, my Cadwal, is really Arviragus, your younger Princely son. He, sir, was wrapped in a most skillfully wrought mantle, created by the hand of his Queen mother, which for more evidence I can with ease produce. This additional evidence will help prove that what I am saying is true."

Cymbeline said, "Guiderius had on his neck a mole, a blood-colored star. It was a birthmark of wonder."

"This is he," Belarius said. "He still has on him that natural stamp. Wise nature gave him that birthmark so that it would now serve as evidence of his identity."

"What! Am I a mother to the birth of three children?" Cymbeline said. "Never has a mother rejoiced over delivery more than I do now."

He said to his two sons, "May you be blessed. For a long time, you have been removed from your places at court, but may you now reign in them!"

He said to his daughter, "Oh, Imogen, you have lost a Kingdom by this finding of your two brothers."

Daughters inherited the crown only when no sons existed or if existing sons were not able to inherit it.

"No, my lord," Imogen replied. "I have gotten two worlds — two brothers — by it."

She then said to Guiderius and Arviragus, "Oh, my gentle brothers, have we really met here? Oh, never say hereafter that I am not the truest speaker of us three. You called me brother, when I was really your sister; I called you brothers, when you were indeed my brothers."

"Have you three met?" Cymbeline asked.

Arviragus replied, "Yes, my good lord."

Guiderius added, "And at first meeting we loved him — our sister — and we continued to love him — our sister — until we thought he — our sister — died."

Doctor Cornelius said, "She appeared to die because she swallowed a small portion of the Queen's potion."

"Oh, rare instinct!" Cymbeline said. "Brothers and sister immediately loved each other although they did not know that they were related!

"When shall I hear everything in detail? I have heard only a severely short summary of a story that has parts that are full of details I do not yet know.

"Imogen, where did you meet your brothers? How did you live? When did you come to serve our Roman captive: Caius Lucius? How did you part from your brothers? How did you first meet them? Why did you flee from the court and where did you go?

"These questions, and the reasons that Belarius and my two sons decided to fight in the battle, and I don't know how many more questions, should be asked, and I should ask about all the other side issues, from event to event, but this time and this place are not suitable for the long question-and-answer session we will have later.

"Look, Posthumus anchors upon — holds tight to — Imogen, and she, like harmless lightning, directs her eye at her husband, her brother, me, and her master, Caius Lucius, looking at each person with joy. And everyone else does as Imogen does.

"Let's leave this ground, and fill the temple with smoke from our sacrifices."

He said to Belarius, "You are my brother."

Using the royal plural, he said, "We'll regard you as our brother forever."

Imogen said to Belarius, "You are my father, too, and you assisted me with the result that I can see this gracious season."

"All are overjoyed," Cymbeline said, "except these captives who are in bonds. Let them be joyful, too, because they shall taste our mercy."

Imogen said to Caius Lucius, "My good master, I will yet do you service."

"May you be happy!" he replied.

Cymbeline said, "The peasant soldier, who so nobly fought in the front ranks, would have well become this place. I would like to give him words of gratitude from a King."

Posthumus said, "I am, sir, the soldier who fought beside these three — Belarius, Guiderius, and Arviragus — and who had an appearance of poverty. It was a fit disguise for the goal I then had.

"Iachimo, say that I was that man. I had you down and might have killed you."

Iachimo had not recognized Posthumus during the battle. Now he realized that Posthumus must have been the peasant soldier because Posthumus knew that the peasant soldier had defeated him and could have killed him.

Iachimo knelt and said, "I am down again, but now my heavy conscience makes my knee sink, just as your strength made my knee sink in the battle. Take that life, I beg you, which I so many times owe you because of my misdeeds, but let me give you back your ring first, and also the bracelet of the truest Princess who ever swore her faithfulness to a husband."

"Don't kneel to me," Posthumus replied. "The power that I have over you is to spare your life, and the 'malice' that I have towards you is to forgive you. Live, and deal with others better in the future."

"Nobly judged!" Cymbeline said. "We'll learn generosity from our son-in-law. Pardon's the word to all our Roman captives."

Arviragus said to Posthumus, "You helped us in the battle, sir, as if you meant indeed to be our brother-in-law. We rejoice that in fact you are our brother-in-law."

Posthumus replied, "I am your servant, Princes."

He said to Caius Lucius, "My good lord of Rome, call forth your soothsayer. As I slept, I thought that great Jupiter, riding on the back of his eagle, appeared to me, with some spritely and ghostly shows of my own dead relatives. When I awakened, I found this tablet lying on my chest. Its content is so difficult that I cannot understand it. Let your soothsayer show his skill by interpreting it."

"Philarmonus!" Caius Lucius called.

Philarmonus the soothsayer replied, "Here I am, my good lord."

"Read the tablet, and explain its meaning."

The soothsayer read the tablet out loud:

"When a lion's whelp shall, to himself unknown, without seeking find, and be embraced by a piece of tender air; and when from a stately cedar shall be lopped branches, which, being dead many years, shall afterward revive, be joined to the old stock and freshly grow, then Posthumus shall end his miseries, and Britain shall be fortunate and flourish in peace and plenty."

He then said to Posthumus, "You, Leonatus, are the lion's whelp — the lion's young. The fit and apt construction of your name *Leonatus*, which is Latin for 'born from a lion,' shows this."

He then said to Cymbeline, "The 'piece of tender air' is your virtuous daughter, Imogen. *Mollis aer* is Latin for 'tender air,' and it is a near homonym for *mulier*, Latin for 'woman,' and Imogen is a masterpiece of a woman."

He said to Posthumus, "Imogen is a very loyal woman, who, just now, in accordance with the letter of the oracle, embraced you. You thought she was dead, so you did not seek her, but you found her without looking for her, and she embraced you."

"This interpretation makes sense," Cymbeline said.

The soothsayer said to King Cymbeline, "The lofty cedar, royal Cymbeline, symbolizes you, and your lopped branches are your two sons. They were stolen by Belarius and for many years were thought to be dead, but they are now revived and joined again to you, the majestic cedar, and your children promise peace and plenty to Britain."

"This is good," Cymbeline said. "We will begin by promoting peace. Caius Lucius, although we are the victors of the battle, we submit to Caesar Augustus and to the Roman Empire. We promise to pay our usual, accustomed tribute, which our wicked Queen persuaded us to not pay. The Heavens justly have laid a heavy hand both on her and on Cloten, her son."

The soothsayer said, "The fingers of the powers above tune the harmony of this peace. The vision that I revealed to Caius Lucius before the beginning stroke of this yet scarcely cold battle is at this instant fully accomplished. My vision was that the Roman eagle, soaring aloft and traveling from south to west on its wings, seemed to grow smaller as it flew and eventually vanished in the beams of the Sun. This vision foreshowed that our Princely eagle, the imperial Caesar Augustus, would again unite his favor with the radiant Cymbeline, who shines here in the west."

"Let us praise the gods," Cymbeline said, "and let our curling smoke climb to their nostrils from the sacrifices on our blest altars. We publicly pronounce news of this peace to all our subjects. Let us go forward. Let a Roman flag and a British flag wave friendly together as we march through Lud's town. In the temple of great Jupiter, we'll ratify our peace and we will seal it with feasts.

"Let's go! Never was there a war that did cease, before bloody hands were washed, with such a peace."

Appendix A: About the Author

It was a dark and stormy night. Suddenly a cry rang out, and on a hot summer night in 1954, Josephine, wife of Carl Bruce, gave birth to a boy — me. Unfortunately, this young married couple allowed Reuben Saturday, Josephine's brother, to name their first-born. Reuben, aka "The Joker," decided that Bruce was a nice name, so he decided to name me Bruce Bruce. I have gone by my middle name — David — ever since.

Being named Bruce David Bruce hasn't been all bad. Bank tellers remember me very quickly, so I don't often have to show an ID. It can be fun in charades, also. When I was a counselor as a teenager at Camp Echoing Hills in Warsaw, Ohio, a fellow counselor gave the signs for "sounds like" and "two words," then she pointed to a bruise on her leg twice. Bruise Bruise? Oh yeah, Bruce Bruce is the answer!

Uncle Reuben, by the way, gave me a haircut when I was in kindergarten. He cut my hair short and shaved a small bald spot on the back of my head. My mother wouldn't let me go to school until the bald spot grew out again.

Of all my brothers and sisters (six in all), I am the only transplant to Athens, Ohio. I was born in Newark, Ohio, and have lived all around Southeastern Ohio. However, I moved to Athens to go to Ohio University and have never left.

At Ohio U, I never could make up my mind whether to major in English or Philosophy, so I got a bachelor's degree with a double major in both areas, then I added a master's degree in English and a master's degree in Philosophy.

Currently, and for a long time to come (I eat fruits and vegetables), I am spending my retirement writing books such as *Nadia Comaneci: Perfect 10*, *The Funniest People in Dance*, *Homer's* Iliad: *A Retelling in Prose*, and *William Shakespeare's* Othello: *A Retelling in Prose*.

By the way, my sister Brenda Kennedy writes romances such as *A New Beginning* and *Shattered Dreams*.

Appendix B: Some Books by David Bruce

Retellings of a Classic Work of Literature

Arden of Faversham: *A Retelling*

Ben Jonson's The Alchemist: *A Retelling*

Ben Jonson's The Arraignment, or Poetaster: *A Retelling*

Ben Jonson's Bartholomew Fair: *A Retelling*

Ben Jonson's The Case is Altered: *A Retelling*

Ben Jonson's Catiline's Conspiracy: *A Retelling*

Ben Jonson's The Devil is an Ass: *A Retelling*

Ben Jonson's Epicene: *A Retelling*

Ben Jonson's Every Man in His Humor: *A Retelling*

Ben Jonson's Every Man Out of His Humor: *A Retelling*

Ben Jonson's The Fountain of Self-Love, or Cynthia's Revels: *A Retelling*

Ben Jonson's The Magnetic Lady, or Humors Reconciled: *A Retelling*

Ben Jonson's The New Inn, or The Light Heart: *A Retelling*

Ben Jonson's Sejanus' Fall: *A Retelling*

Ben Jonson's The Staple of News: *A Retelling*

Ben Jonson's A Tale of a Tub: *A Retelling*

Ben Jonson's Volpone, or the Fox: *A Retelling*

Christopher Marlowe's Complete Plays: Retellings

Christopher Marlowe's Dido, Queen of Carthage: *A Retelling*

Christopher Marlowe's Doctor Faustus: *Retellings of the 1604 A-Text and of the 1616 B-Text*

Christopher Marlowe's Edward II: *A Retelling*

Christopher Marlowe's The Massacre at Paris: *A Retelling*

Christopher Marlowe's The Rich Jew of Malta: *A Retelling*

Christopher Marlowe's Tamburlaine, Parts 1 and 2: *Retellings*

Dante's Divine Comedy: *A Retelling in Prose*

Dante's Inferno: *A Retelling in Prose*

Dante's Purgatory: *A Retelling in Prose*

Dante's Paradise: *A Retelling in Prose*

The Famous Victories of Henry V: *A Retelling*

From the Iliad *to the* Odyssey: *A Retelling in Prose of Quintus of Smyrna's* Posthomerica

George Chapman, Ben Jonson, and John Marston's Eastward Ho! *A Retelling*

George Peele's The Arraignment of Paris: *A Retelling*

George Peele's The Battle of Alcazar: *A Retelling*

George Peele's David and Bathsheba, and the Tragedy of Absalom: *A Retelling*

George Peele's Edward I: *A Retelling*

George Peele's The Old Wives' Tale: *A Retelling*

George-a-Greene: *A Retelling*

The History of King Leir: *A Retelling*

Homer's Iliad: *A Retelling in Prose*

Homer's Odyssey: *A Retelling in Prose*

J.W. Gent.'s The Valiant Scot: *A Retellings*

Jason and the Argonauts: A Retelling in Prose of Apollonius of Rhodes' Argonautica

John Ford: Eight Plays Translated into Modern English

John Ford's The Broken Heart: *A Retelling*

John Ford's The Fancies, Chaste and Noble: *A Retelling*

John Ford's The Lady's Trial: *A Retelling*

John Ford's The Lover's Melancholy: *A Retelling*

John Ford's Love's Sacrifice: *A Retelling*

John Ford's Perkin Warbeck: *A Retelling*

John Ford's The Queen: *A Retelling*

John Ford's 'Tis Pity She's a Whore: *A Retelling*

John Lyly's Campaspe: *A Retelling*

John Lyly's Endymion, The Man in the Moon: *A Retelling*

John Lyly's Galatea: *A Retelling*

John Lyly's Love's Metamorphosis: *A Retelling*

John Lyly's Midas: *A Retelling*

John Lyly's Mother Bombie: *A Retelling*

John Lyly's Sappho and Phao: *A Retelling*

John Lyly's The Woman in the Moon: *A Retelling*

John Webster's The White Devil: *A Retelling*

King Edward III: *A Retelling*

Mankind: *A Medieval Morality Play* (A Retelling)

Margaret Cavendish's The Unnatural Tragedy: *A Retelling*

The Merry Devil of Edmonton: *A Retelling*

The Summoning of Everyman: *A Medieval Morality Play* (A Retelling)

Robert Greene's Friar Bacon and Friar Bungay: *A Retelling*

The Taming of a Shrew: *A Retelling*

Tarlton's Jests: A Retelling

Thomas Middleton's A Chaste Maid in Cheapside: *A Retelling*

Thomas Middleton's Women Beware Women: *A Retelling*

Thomas Middleton and Thomas Dekker's The Roaring Girl: *A Retelling*

Thomas Middleton and William Rowley's The Changeling: *A Retelling*

The Trojan War and Its Aftermath: Four Ancient Epic Poems

Virgil's Aeneid: *A Retelling in Prose*

William Shakespeare's 5 Late Romances: Retellings in Prose

William Shakespeare's 10 Histories: Retellings in Prose

William Shakespeare's 11 Tragedies: Retellings in Prose

William Shakespeare's 12 Comedies: Retellings in Prose

William Shakespeare's 38 Plays: Retellings in Prose

William Shakespeare's 1 Henry IV, aka Henry IV, Part 1: *A Retelling in Prose*

William Shakespeare's 2 Henry IV, aka Henry IV, Part 2: *A Retelling in Prose*

William Shakespeare's 1 Henry VI, aka Henry VI, Part 1: *A Retelling in Prose*

William Shakespeare's 2 Henry VI, aka Henry VI, Part 2: *A Retelling in Prose*

William Shakespeare's 3 Henry VI, aka Henry VI, Part 3: *A Retelling in Prose*

William Shakespeare's All's Well that Ends Well: *A Retelling in Prose*

William Shakespeare's Antony and Cleopatra: *A Retelling in Prose*

William Shakespeare's As You Like It: *A Retelling in Prose*

William Shakespeare's The Comedy of Errors: *A Retelling in Prose*

William Shakespeare's Coriolanus: *A Retelling in Prose*

William Shakespeare's Cymbeline: *A Retelling in Prose*

William Shakespeare's Hamlet: *A Retelling in Prose*

William Shakespeare's Henry V: *A Retelling in Prose*

William Shakespeare's Henry VIII: *A Retelling in Prose*

William Shakespeare's Julius Caesar: *A Retelling in Prose*

William Shakespeare's King John: *A Retelling in Prose*

William Shakespeare's King Lear: *A Retelling in Prose*

William Shakespeare's Love's Labor's Lost: *A Retelling in Prose*

William Shakespeare's Macbeth: *A Retelling in Prose*

William Shakespeare's Measure for Measure: *A Retelling in Prose*

William Shakespeare's The Merchant of Venice: *A Retelling in Prose*

William Shakespeare's The Merry Wives of Windsor: *A Retelling in Prose*

William Shakespeare's A Midsummer Night's Dream: *A Retelling in Prose*

William Shakespeare's Much Ado About Nothing: *A Retelling in Prose*

William Shakespeare's Othello: *A Retelling in Prose*

William Shakespeare's Pericles, Prince of Tyre: *A Retelling in Prose*

William Shakespeare's Richard II: *A Retelling in Prose*

William Shakespeare's Richard III: *A Retelling in Prose*

William Shakespeare's Romeo and Juliet: *A Retelling in Prose*

William Shakespeare's The Taming of the Shrew: *A Retelling in Prose*

William Shakespeare's The Tempest: *A Retelling in Prose*

William Shakespeare's Timon of Athens: *A Retelling in Prose*

William Shakespeare's Titus Andronicus: *A Retelling in Prose*

William Shakespeare's Troilus and Cressida: *A Retelling in Prose*

William Shakespeare's Twelfth Night: *A Retelling in Prose*

William Shakespeare's The Two Gentlemen of Verona: *A Retelling in Prose*

William Shakespeare's The Two Noble Kinsmen: *A Retelling in Prose*

William Shakespeare's The Winter's Tale: *A Retelling in Prose*